TWO STRIKES ON LEFTY

TWO STRIKES ON LEFTY

By JOSEPH A. MOORE

Illustrations and Jacket by
HAROLD CUE

W. A. Wilde Company Publishers
Boston, Massachusetts

Copyright, 1954
By W. A. WILDE COMPANY
All rights reserved

TWO STRIKES ON LEFTY

Library of Congress Catalog Card No. 54-10626

MADE IN THE UNITED STATES OF AMERICA

dedicated to
everyone who likes baseball

CONTENTS

CHAPTER	PAGE
1. "Don't Come Back If You Fail!"	11
2. Fairmount—Last in the Valley League	26
3. Clothesline Hitter	35
4. That Terrible Tarbin Temper	45
5. Winter in Florida	60
6. Tom Silk Returns	73
7. Home, Sweet Home, in Idaho	84
8. Pepper-Pot Infield	101
9. SOS to Bobby Dale	117
10. Oh, You Roughnecks!	129
11. Fifteen Thousand Rabbits' Feet	142
12. Out of the Tiger Chain	161
13. Action at Parker Field	170
14. Hello, Fenway Park!	183
15. Surprise for Lefty	194
16. Good-bye, Tarbin Temper	208

LIST OF ILLUSTRATIONS

	PAGE
Frontispiece	
The umpire's right arm jerked up	115
The throw bounced out of Lefty's crab-net	200

CHAPTER I

"DON'T COME BACK IF YOU FAIL!"

A BRIGHT morning sun streamed across the campus of Bolton College and in through the windows of Leverett Dormitory. In one of the dormitory rooms, a tall youth with straw-colored hair sat on a pile of books between two beds. With a smooth, easy motion he honed the baseball bat in his hands, using a piece of fine sandpaper. A small can of machine oil stood on the floor nearby.

The youth put the sandpaper down, raised the bat, and squinted along its surface. Then he poured a little more oil on the sandpaper and began honing again.

He was patiently rubbing away when the door opened and three other fellows about his own age walked in. The first one was stocky and dark, with keen black eyes.

"Hi, Lefty!" the newcomer, who was Lefty's roommate, said. Then, when he saw what Lefty was doing, he chuckled, "Wassa matter? Hole in the bat?"

Lefty started to flush, but caught himself and grinned.

"The bat's not smooth," he said. "It has got to be smooth for this afternoon's game. Even a second baseman like you should know that, Bobby."

The two others filed in behind Bobby. One was slight of build and moved lazily. The other, stolid and husky, stayed near the door.

The lazy one said, "Why smooth, Lefty? Is our favorite first baseman planning on doin' something with the bat today?"

Lefty tightened his lips and a quick flash came into his hazel eyes. "Look, Ed Sinsibaugh," he growled. "I happen to be the leading batter this year for Bolton. You're a .250 hitting shortstop, but you keep ribbing me about my base hits. What's the idea?"

Ed grinned more widely and chuckled, "Temper, temper!"

Bobby Dale said quickly, "That's just it, Lefty. Anybody starts kidding you, an' you get hot under the collar. That could hurt, in a ball game. They'll just say, get Lefty Tarbin sore and he'll blow the game."

Lefty got up, put the bat on the dresser, and col-

"*Don't Come Back if You Fail!*" 13

lected the pile of books. He shoved the sandpaper and the can of machine oil into a drawer.

He said, "All I know is, you play a ball game to win. That's the only way I know how to play. How about you guys?"

They all became serious and nodded. Stan Homek, the husky one near the door, who played third base, spoke for the first time. "You're right, Lefty. But remember, don't let the State guys get your goat today!"

"I won't, Stan," Lefty promised. "Seeing it's our last game for Bolton—the last game for us infielders, anyway—I want to win it as much as you do."

That afternoon came as bright and clear as the morning had indicated. When the Bolton players trotted onto their home diamond, the stands were packed. Except for the slightest suggestion of a breeze, the air was calm and quiet.

State University's team went through its practice, alternating with Bolton in the batting cage. Then Bolton, spic and span in their violet-trimmed uniforms, went onto the field for the final pre-game drill.

Lefty, taking the other infielders' warm-up throws, felt keyed up by pride in his team as well as by the fact that this was his last game for Bolton. Across the diamond at third, Stan Homek, silent but dependable, scooped up a practice grounder and shot a low, underhand throw to first. Lefty grabbed it and tossed back to Coach Fred Carey at the plate.

The coach sent a hot drive on the turf to Ed Sinsibaugh. The lazy-appearing shortstop actually was anything but slow. He faded easily to his right, gloved the hot shot, and sent it to Lefty almost in one motion.

"That's fielding," Lefty grunted to himself. "Maybe you can't hit much, Ed, but you sure can come up outta the dirt with 'em."

Coach hit the last one to Bobby Dale at second. The umpire talked briefly with both coaches, took their opening lineups, and yelled, "Play ball!"

For six innings it was a slow game. Nobody scored for either team, while the opposing pitchers handled the ball as carefully as if it were dynamite. Ace Brillon, the Bolton hurler, gave the State batters little but a curve ball they could not hit. But neither could Bolton get a man beyond first base.

Then in the sixth inning, trouble started. A State batter hit a long single to deep right with one out. When Bolton's right fielder briefly juggled the ball, the Statesman shot off for second. The play was terrifically close, but the base umpire flattened his palms downward, and State's fans erupted in a bedlam of joy.

As the next batter stood at the plate, knocking the dirt from his cleats with a bat, Lefty started to

"Don't Come Back if You Fail!"

move in on the infield dirt. He pounded his left fist lightly in his crab-net mitt.

The State runner kicked the dirt restlessly off second base, and his coach at third yelled something to him. If this batter hit safely, Lefty thought grimly, that run was in the bag for State.

"Bear down, Ace, bear down!" Stan Homek yelled.

Ed Sinsibaugh, Bolton's holler guy, faked a move behind the runner, and then stopped abruptly to shout encouragement to his pitcher. "Pour it down his throat, Ace . . . heads up, guys!"

Lefty glanced down the base line toward Bobby Dale. Bobby was smooth and efficient, but not a gabby guy. He tried to talk it up with the rest of the infield. But, as Lefty often said, Bobby did most of his talking with glove and bat.

Despite the tension, Lefty smiled to himself as he waited for Ace to pitch. This was the kind of ball team he liked to be on. This was playing baseball to the limit, the way he liked it.

Suddenly his hazel eyes narrowed, and the smile faded from his lips. Burly Sam Greaves behind the plate was holding one finger pointing down. Lefty recognized the signal. A fast ball, outside, to the right-handed State hitter. If the batter connected, the ball probably would come down Lefty's side of the diamond, travelling fast.

Lefty moved back and toward the foul line. The rest of the infield shifted with him. Wind raised a sudden cloud of dust over the base paths, and Lefty saw the State runner cover his eyes and hustle back toward second. He drew his own hand across his mouth to wipe away the flying dirt. The flat taste of lime dust from the foul line came into his mouth. Silence lay over the field for a moment as the gust of wind petered out.

Ace Brillon raised his pitching arm, brought it down like a buggy whip across his body, and fired the ball plateward. Lefty's eyes scarcely could follow the white blur, and he knew how the batter must feel. But the State hitter refused to budge an inch. He swung his bat in a smooth, powerful motion, and wood cracked sharply against horsehide.

It was a late swing. Sam had called for the correct pitch. No right-handed batter could ever get around in time to pull Ace's smoke ball to left field. But if it went safely into right—

Comet-like, the ball blazed a path down the first-base line. It crossed the bag over the inside corner, roaring between Lefty and the foul line without losing speed. For one desperate instant he saw the white streak flashing by. Then he lunged, stuck out his crab-net, and speared the line drive inches before it hit the ground.

He straightened up and threw the ball, almost without looking. He knew Ed Sinsibaugh had broken for second with Ace's pitch. Good old Ed! Sure enough, he was there, perched expectantly on the bag to take Lefty's throw. The Statesman,

"Don't Come Back if You Fail!"

already half-way home on the apparent hit, easily was doubled out.

Lefty chuckled as Ed let out a Comanche war whoop. Bolton players trotted toward the bench, throwing their gloves onto the grass behind the infield.

"How to go, Lefty!" Ed chortled gleefully. "You still got glue in that mitt, huh?"

Cheers rolled over the diamond from the packed Bolton stands.

"Yea, Lefty! Yea, Tarbin!"

Lefty felt a warm glow. He knew it was Sam's smart thinking that had set up the double play. He himself had merely gone through the motions. But it had been a smooth, fast piece of glove work, and he felt good inside.

The game dragged into the ninth inning without a score.

Then, in the top of the ninth, with one out, State's Jim Barry beat out a slow roller to Stan Homek. Barry was lightning on the base paths, and if he reached second, State would have a good chance to score. Lefty, feet against the bag, held up his crab-net as a target for Ace to try to pick Barry off.

Ace threw a waste ball, high and wide. Barry refused to steal. He danced back and forth off first, waving his arms, insulting Ace, trying to rattle him. Ace threw once to Lefty, but Barry slid safely under the tag.

Ace uncorked another wide pitch. Barry started for second, halted, then ran back. Sam will never miss this chance, Lefty figured. He was right. When the Bolton catcher saw Barry stop momentarily, he rifled a throw to first.

The play should have been duck soup. But Barry refused to be a sitting duck. When he saw himself trapped, he came driving back, spikes high and flashing in the sunlight.

The sharp steel bit cruelly into Lefty's ankle. He felt it dig into the bone. It seemed that Barry deliberately spiked him, drawing the knife-like steel viciously across his flesh. Despite the biting pain, he tagged Barry with the ball as hard as he could. The State runner retaliated by bringing up his left knee into Lefty's stomach.

That did it. Lefty saw red. He lunged and hit Barry in the mouth. Instantly both players were rolling and punching over the infield dirt.

The stands became a near-bedlam. Partisan Bolton rooters yelled for Barry's blood. To prevent serious trouble, players on both teams assisted the umpire in separating the fighters.

"You're both outta the game!" the man in blue snapped when the fighting ceased.

Lefty, snarling like a wildcat, tried to protest. "He spiked me! You saw him give me the knee!"

"You're both outta the game," the umpire repeated shortly.

Barry walked off, mumbling. Lefty hesitated. He

"Don't Come Back if You Fail!"

wanted to continue his protest. Then he felt a hand on his arm. It was his coach, Fred Carey.

Lefty said, "You saw him knee me, Coach."

Carey nodded. "Yeah. But you tagged him out, so you shoulda let it go." He eyed Lefty briefly. "You're outta the game, anyway. If you're not careful, that temper of yours is gonna cause you plenty of trouble. Get Shorty to fix up that ankle."

Lefty limped to the dressing room, where Shorty, the trainer, daubed his ankle with iodine. The gash was not deep. After a shower, he had simmered down; but still inside he felt that he had been given a raw deal. Since he was a senior, and the State contest closed Bolton's schedule, this was the last college game he would ever play. Well, if that was the way they handled college baseball, he was glad to quit. He had enough of it.

Loud cheering burst from the field. Then Walt Billings, student manager, came into the locker room shouting that Bolton had won the game in the tenth, one to nothing, on Bobby Dale's home run.

Lefty went to his dormitory room before the others came off the field. He was there, his long, lean form stretched across the bed, when Bobby Dale opened the door. Bobby grinned sympathetically as he walked in.

"Sorry you got bounced, pal. But heck, it's all in the game."

Lefty said tonelessly, "I guess so." Then his hazel

eyes brightened. "Congratulations on your home run, Bobby."

The door opened again. Ed Sinsibaugh and Stan Homek crowded into the room. "Here we are," Stan rumbled in his heavy voice. "The last meetin' of the million-dollar infield."

Ed chuckled. "A million-dollar infield that doesn't know where it will eat, week after next."

Three faces took on a sober cast. Ed had voiced a thought that weighed on three minds. Lefty alone could be sure of a job. His father owned a construction and lumber business in Idaho. All Lefty had to do was go home and start work.

"It's not as easy as that," Lefty said, when his assured future was pointed out by the others.

Bobby's dark eyes widened slightly. "Why not?"

"I'm not going into Dad's business."

"Then what'll you do?" Stan queried. "You gotta work somewhere."

"You can't eat fresh air the way you been eatin' up ground balls the past four years," Ed Sinsibaugh wise-cracked.

Lefty ran long fingers through his straw-colored hair and half-grinned. "No, I can't live on fresh air alone. Nor on the umpire's hot air, either," he agreed, thinking darkly of that day's run-in with the umpire. "I may stay alive, though, if I can keep eatin' up those ground balls Ed mentioned."

They looked puzzled. Ed said, "What you mean by that, Lefty?"

"Don't Come Back if You Fail!"

Lefty shifted his lengthy form on the bed. "I mean I've made up my mind what I'm going to do for a living."

"Well, unload the secret."

Lefty paused before he answered. He enjoyed the mild drama of the moment. "I'm going to play professional baseball."

Bobby came bolt upright. "No!" His dark eyes held a look of disbelief.

Stan grunted, "You're kiddin', of course."

Lefty shook his head.

"Your old man," Ed pointed out, "can pay you six times what you'll get in pro ball."

"You're a good ball player, Lefty, but no one ever can be sure of making the major league grade," Stan argued. "An' life in the minors, the way I hear it, is hardly worth livin'."

Bobby cleared his throat and spoke carefully. "There's one more thing. You have a—well, a pretty quick temper, Lefty." Lefty started to flush; but Bobby, having begun, went on quickly. "I've heard it's mighty tough for hot-headed men in baseball. Plenty of 'em have been ridden out of the game because they blew up so often and so easily."

"Maybe so," Lefty replied curtly. "But I'll have to take that chance."

Bobby continued relentlessly. He was Lefty's best friend. Otherwise he would not have dared speak so frankly. But he would not have wished to see Lefty end up as a broken-down tramp athlete, either.

"How about your father? I happen to know that he, for some strange reason, hates baseball, and even objected to your playing at Bolton. I understand he once said he would disown any son of his that became a professional ball player. Any way you look at it, Lefty, if you go into baseball for pay, you've got two strikes on you before you start."

Lefty said thoughtfully, "Maybe you're right about those two strikes, Bobby. I dunno. But I've got something else, too."

He reached into the top right drawer of the mission desk beside the bed. When his hand came out, it held a legal-looking piece of folded paper. He handed it to Bobby. "Read that."

Bobby, unfolding the paper, glanced quickly through its contents. Then he whistled softly. "Golly, you've done it, Lefty! It's a contract, guys! A contract to play ball this summer with the Fairmount team in the Valley League."

"That's a class C league," Ed said quickly.

Stan grunted. "Hmm. Not bad, Lefty. Not a bad place to start, if you're set on bein' a pro."

"My mind's made up."

Bobby folded the contract and handed it back. "Then all we can do is wish you luck." He offered his hand. So did the others. "Just one thing, though. Have you told your dad?"

"Don't Come Back if You Fail!"

Lefty paused a moment. "Not yet," he said. "I'm going downstairs now to phone him, long distance. I'd wait until commencement day, but he can't be here. Pressure of business. And Mom won't make the trip alone."

In the phone booth, while the others lounged outside, Lefty put in the long-distance call. He waited until the call went through. Then his father's familiar, deep tones came over the wire.

"Hello, Lefty! Glad to hear your voice. Sorry we can't get to the commencement. But I'm busy as a one-armed hod carrier here. And your ma won't go alone." The heavy voice paused briefly, and Lefty guessed what was coming. "I need you here, Lefty. Lots of construction work going on. Hope you'll be home to go to work soon."

A trickle of sweat ran down Lefty's back. This was going to be rough. But somehow the words came out.

"Look, Dad . . . about the job. I'm afraid . . . well, I just can't take it."

"What!"

Lefty felt the explosion coming over the wire. Momentarily he had a ridiculous thought. He hoped the telephone operator did not have a new hair-do, for if she had the ear-phones on, his dad's fiery anger would surely burn her hair off.

Then the hot words from the other end came crackling through again. "What do you mean, you can't take it? You're goin' to work, aren't you? If you don't come here for a job, what do you think you'll do?"

That question gave Lefty his chance.

"I'm going to play professional baseball, Dad. I've just signed a contract with a team in class C."

There was a long silence. Lefty could imagine the thoughts that were racing through his father's mind on the other end. He expected another big explosion.

But the words that came through were quiet— ominously quiet. They had the ring of a determined man who spoke with finality.

"You're of age to do what you want, Lefty. I can't stop you. You ought to be old enough to know what you're doing. But let me tell you one thing . . . if you fail in baseball, don't come back here. There will be no job waiting for you with me. Good-bye!"

The receiver clicked on the other end. The conversation was over.

Lefty hung up and slowly left the booth. Anxious looks showed on the faces of his three friends. He told them what his father had said as they went back upstairs.

Ed asked, "What's the reason he hates baseball so?"

Lefty sighed. "I dunno. But he won't go to a game, read about one, or listen on the radio. I never even played much until I went away to prep school."

"Seems unreasonable," Stan said, "but I s'pose you gotta face it. Probably he has a reason. When do you report to Fairmount?"

"Right after commencement. There's a train from here the next morning. It gets there about midnight."

Bobby said, "Gosh, Lefty, think you'll bust into the lineup right away?"

"Dunno. But if I do, guys, I sure hope I have as swell an infield with me as this million-dollar Bolton one!"

He ducked the pillow that Ed Sinsibaugh hurled at him.

CHAPTER II

FAIRMOUNT—
LAST IN THE VALLEY LEAGUE

LEFTY stared out the dirt-streaked train window at the low afternoon sun. He had been riding all day and was feeling cramped. But his physical discomfort was nothing compared to the excitement he felt inside. Butterflies seemed constantly to be fluttering around in his stomach.

The nearer he got to Fairmount, the more uncertain he felt. Not uncertain or doubtful about his choice of professional baseball as a career. His natural stubbornness never would have let him go back on that decision. But uncertainty as to whether he could climb to the top in one of the most competitive fields in existence.

In professional baseball, he knew, many are tested, but very few achieve major league stardom. For every Ted Williams, there are hundreds of forgotten Joe Smiths; for every Bobby Feller or Ralph Kiner, scores of disappointed youths drift back to the sandlots each year.

But I, Lefty Tarbin, don't intend to fail!

He stirred in his seat and smiled to himself. That was just what he had said to his Bolton pals when he left them. The other three had caught an express for New York. Ed Sinsibaugh lived on Long Island, Stan Homek's folks had a small grocery store in Manhattan, and Bobby Dale was headed back to his father's farm in northern Maine.

The train made a depot stop, and a stout man came aboard and took the seat beside Lefty. The man rattled his newspaper, coughed, and said: "Goin' far, young man?"

Lefty, startled, looked up.

The stout man smiled engagingly. "I thought since we are both travelin' together at the moment, you might like some conversation."

Lefty said, "Sure." He did not feel much like talking; but he suspected that the stranger wanted to talk more than listen, so he said, "Sure," again.

The stout man rambled on, Lefty half-listening. Then some of the words caught his attention.

"Yes, sirree!" his companion was saying. "If a man wants to get someplace, he's gotta have drive. Won't get anywhere if he goes at a thing halfhearted. Now take me. If I hadn't made up my mind twenty years ago that I'd become the best gosh-darned salesman in my territory, where'd I be now? Right back in Four Corners, clerking in Sam Parker's general store. Yes, sirree, that's where." Abruptly he paused. "Say, where you goin'?"

Lefty hesitated. He'd rather not reveal that he was a ball player, for he did not feel like answering the dozens of questions his seatmate would surely ask. So he said tersely, "Got a chance at a business job in Fairmount."

"Good!" the other said. "Now listen to me. Make up your mind that nothin'—nothin' whatever!—will stop you from makin' good. Have reasons for makin' good. If there ain't reasons, get some! Maybe it's a girl—or you wanta make some money—or to prove somethin' to somebody. Whatever it is, get a reason. An' if you keep that in mind all the time"—he tapped Lefty on the knee—"you'll make the grade. You just can't help it!"

Lefty almost could hear the stout man add, "Like me!" Later the cocky passenger got off, leaving Lefty with the admonition to "find a reason to be successful—and you will be!"

At first Lefty was inclined to laugh and forget the man. But, he reflected, just what are my own reasons for wanting to make good? There wasn't any girl; not yet, at least. True, everyone wanted to make good, just on general principles. But what exact goal have I got?

Suddenly, as he stared into the swift-gathering dusk, he got the answer. It was not only success for its own sake that he wanted. It was his love for playing baseball, his desire to make the game his life, that drove him on. And, growing out of that, was the wish to prove to his father that his hatred for baseball was all wrong. If he could do that, if he could bring his dad to see that when he knew the game he, too, would love it, then Lefty as a successful player would have as sweet a double triumph as anyone could want.

When he reached Fairmount, the depot clock showed eleven-fifteen. His orders were to go directly to the team's hotel when he arrived and to wait until morning before reporting at the ball park. So he hailed a cab, rode to the hotel, and turned in without seeing anyone but the desk clerk.

Next morning, after a good sleep, he felt refreshed. He ate breakfast in the hotel. He had heard absolutely no mention of the Fairmount ball team since his arrival, and wondered if there was any local interest in the club.

He thought, "Maybe this isn't exactly a red-hot baseball city."

Idly he turned the pages of a local newspaper. He found the sports section, and ran his eye quickly over the page for some mention of the club. There should be a write-up somewhere.

He found it, buried down in an inside corner. The small-type headline read, "BEAVERS LOSE EIGHTH STRAIGHT." The story beneath could hardly be called a friendly one. The reporter had written:

"This gets monotonous. Yesterday afternoon the unbusy Beavers did it again. Lost another ball game, that is. They were shut out at Beaver Park, 6-0, by the Bayville Bombers in a drab, dreary contest. Tod Blue got two of Fairmount's three hits, and Hugo Matthews had the other.

"The Beavers haven't a chance to go anywhere this year. They will stay right in the cellar. Couldn't we expect, though, a little more of the old college try, and some smarter baseball from them?"

There was more of the same, but Lefty did not bother to read it. He knew how poorly a team must be going, and how disgusted a baseball writer must be, to have stories like that appear. Obviously every fan in town was "off" the Beavers, and unless the team could win a few games, it would remain the joke of the circuit.

He discovered the Valley League standings at the bottom of the page. The Beavers were deep in the cellar of the six-team league. Best clubs appeared to be the Bayville Bombers and the Cole City Blue Sox, who stood first and second respectively.

Lefty said to himself, "So this is the team I've signed to play with! If I can't nail down a job here, I might as well quit."

He looked around the dining room, and noticed that several groups of young men had come in. He tabbed them for ball players, but rather than make any contacts now he preferred to wait until he met them at the park. Quietly he left the dining room.

He thought of looking up Cy Benteen, Beaver manager. Then he decided to go out to the park first. He went back to his room, put his baseball shoes, glove, and several other items in a small canvas bag, and came back downstairs. He walked across the lobby, out onto the sidewalk, and hailed a cab.

Usually cabbies are ready and anxious to discuss the local ball team. But this one was actively disinterested. When he dropped Lefty at the park, he didn't even ask if he was a player.

Beaver Park was not much of a stadium. The stands, hardly more than open bleachers, wore a broken-down look, and the grandstand roof appeared ready to collapse. The playing field wasn't too bad, however. Lefty made a mental note that there must be a hard-working groundskeeper, for the grass, though brown and worn, was evenly cut. The base paths looked gravelly, but were fairly smooth compared with some he had seen. Lefty had never played on a major college diamond that was not better than this one, though.

When he turned to look for the manager's office, he found a short, bald man standing quietly beside him. The man had a wide smile on his moon-like face. He stuck out a pudgy hand and said, "Hiya, feller. You look like the new ball player we been expectin'."

"That's right," Lefty said, somehow feeling immediately at ease. "I'm Lefty Tarbin."

The round man's grin widened. "Welcome, Lefty. I'm Shorty Timmins, the trainer."

"Hey!" said Lefty. "That's what we called our trainer at Bolton. Are all you guys named Shorty?"

Shorty's grin became a cackle. "All trainers'

brains is in their feet," he explained. "That's what keeps us from growin' up. We grow down instead. If our brains was in our heads, we'd be managers, not trainers."

He cackled uproariously at his own humor. Lefty liked him even more.

"Come on, I'll take yuh to your locker," Shorty said.

They went into the dressing room. It was a ramshackle place, the benches worn and unpainted, the floor splintered with the marks of a thousand spiked shoes. An acrid smell of liniment hung over the low-ceilinged room. Someone had lately taken a shower, and the air was still damp from steam. But these sights and smells of athletes' quarters were nectar to Lefty, and he felt right at home.

Shorty pointed to a locker. "Dump your stuff in there. I'll take you up to Benteen's office. He's there a'ready, gets in early. When yuh come back I'll have a uniform fer you."

Lefty had time to see a piece of gummed paper, with his last name pencilled on it, stuck to the metal door of the locker. There were remnants of many other gummed pieces there. He hoped his name would not be replaced too soon.

They went up a flight of narrow wooden stairs that creaked at every step. Then there was a door marked "Manager." Just before opening it, Shorty whispered, "Benteen's a grouch. But don't mind him. All yuh have to do is play good baseball."

Fairmount   33

Then he was gone and Lefty found himself standing alone before a small, wizened man with greasy black hair and cold green eyes.

"So you're Tarbin, eh?" Benteen almost snarled. "Been readin' the papers atall?"

"I saw today's *Clarion*," Lefty replied cautiously.

"Read anything 'bout the Beavers?"

Lefty fidgeted. "Yeah. The story of yesterday's game."

"Huh!" Benteen spat. "Them blasted sports writers. They're a mangy bunch." He paused, his cold green eyes filled with hate. He made a breaking motion with clenched fists, as though snapping a baseball writer in two. Finally he went on, "Listen, Tarbin. We got a slow club. No pep. No life atall. Too many washed-up old timers. An' mebbe too many unwashed kids. Our scout signed you. Okay. I'll have to take yuh. But I've had plenty of freshwater college jerks already. Most of 'em are pantywaists. Your contract will protect you for this year. But if yuh don't make good—out you go!"

Lefty's hazel eyes widened. He saw no reason for Benteen's tirade, even before the new first baseman had stepped on the field. He groped for something to say, then decided not to say it.

Benteen tapped a pencil ceaselessly on the desk top. "I want hard hitters, hard runners, an' hard throwers. But no soreheads. No guys that blow up an' throw away ball games . . . Unnerstand? . . . Okay. Get your stuff from Shorty. Better be dressed by twelve-thirty. Game's at two. Bayville's here one more day."

Lefty said, "Thanks, Mr. Benteen," and went out. Between the pencil tapping and the cold green eyes he was beginning to get the willies. And that warning about soreheads. Had someone tipped Benteen off about Lefty's temper?

Shorty was putting a Beaver uniform in Lefty's locker. "How'd yuh like Benteen?" he asked. Then, without waiting for an answer, he went on, "I guess I got everything you need in here."

"Thanks, Shorty. You're a pal. Benteen told me to be dressed at twelve-thirty."

"Good idea. Mosta the boys is on the field by one. Any time after noon yuh wanna make it, I'll get someone to warm up with yuh."

Lefty went toward the door. "Okay. I'll see you."

He walked out onto the street and took a long, deep breath. This was it. This was the moment he had dreamed of for years and years. At last he was playing baseball for a living!

CHAPTER III

CLOTHESLINE HITTER

He stepped onto the Beaver diamond for the first time that day shortly after noon. Hardly a fan sat in the weatherbeaten stands, but several players already were out tossing a ball. One of them called to him.

"Hey, pal, wanna get in some battin' practice?"

"You bet!"

"Then shag a few balls first, and you'll get your turn." The speaker, a rangy, quick-smiling blonde youngster, shook hands as Lefty passed him on the way to the outfield. "I'm Art Gray. Sub outfielder. Been here two weeks. A real veteran, givin' you orders already!"

Here was at least one Beaver whom Lefty knew he would like.

Gray and another youth took turns in the cage and slammed line drives all over the outfield. Lefty chased them without exerting himself. Maybe he would not play today, but he intended to stay fresh and ready. Finally Gray motioned him to come in.

The bat felt good in his hands. He laid wood against several fat pitches, and the hard-hit balls went screaming to the far corners of the park. Several times he hit the distant right-field fence on the fly. A few "ooh's" and "ah's" came from the scattering of slowly arriving bleacherites.

When he finished, he turned and saw Benteen watching him from the runway. Benteen's face was expressionless, and the hard green eyes were cold as ever.

"Hey, you guys," Benteen called. "C'mere. Meetin'."

Inside the clubhouse, Benteen quickly introduced Lefty to the others. Then he gave a five-minute pep talk. His harsh, nasal tones penetrated to every corner of the room, and he spared none of the men in pointing out faults. He went over the Bayville lineup man by man, and showed how each Bomber should be played and pitched to.

Lefty noticed with some satisfaction that Benteen did no crying over spilled milk. Yesterday's game was over, and the runty manager now pointed for today's contest. It was apparent that the man at least knew his baseball.

Benteen finally said, "Okay!" like a movie director yelling, "Cut!" The men rose from the benches and filed out of the clubhouse. Some of the younger players hustled onto the field, but the old-timers took it easy. They did not seem visibly affected by Benteen's talk.

Lefty got his turn at batting practice, but most of the pre-game time he spent shagging flies in the outfield. Finally the Bombers took over for their workout, and Lefty came in to the bench. He sat beside Art Gray. Benteen paid no attention to either of them.

With ten minutes to go, the Beaver infield went out for their final workout. This Lefty wanted to see. He was dying to get a look at the Fairmount inner cordon, especially the first baseman.

"They're not bad," Art Gray said, "not bad atall. But they don't hit consistently. It's the old story. Good field, no hit."

Lefty stared unblinkingly at the diamond. "Who's the first baseman?"

Gray chuckled. "Interested, huh? Well, he's Tod Blue. An old-timer. Been slippin' deeper into the bushes every year. All washed up and knows it."

"Why doesn't he quit, then?"

Gray looked speculatively across the diamond. "For the same reason you and I are tryin' to break in, I s'pose. The guy loves baseball. Eats, sleeps, an' drinks it. He won't quit until they cut that uniform off him."

"Oh!" Lefty felt quick, deep sympathy for Tod Blue. He could guess how the tottering veteran felt.

But the feeling did not alter one bit his determination to take the man's job away from him if he could.

Beaver pitcher Clay Dennis surprised everyone by holding the Bombers scoreless for six innings. Maybe, thought Lefty, Benteen's talk was doing some good. Then, in the seventh, Bayville pushed across a run on a pass, a sacrifice, and a single to right. Dennis had not given up many hits, but his fast ball seemed to be losing its zip.

Through it all Benteen hunched on the bench, never moving a muscle. The Beavers, trailing now by a run, came in for their half of the seventh. With one out, Buster Nash hit a short fly back of second base that dropped in safely.

"You, Gray!" Benteen went into action like a whiplash. "Get out there an' run for Nash."

Art leaped from the bench and hustled to first base. Nash was an old-timer, a slow runner. Art was out there to bring in the tying run. Unfortunately, though, the bottom of the Fairmount batting order was coming up.

Slow-footed Earl McIntyre trudged to the plate. McIntyre, an uninspired catcher, knew that all he had to do was lay down a bunt. He did it, and was thrown out before he got half-way to first. Two outs. But the sacrifice advanced Art to second base.

What would Benteen do now? Lefty had sensed for some time that Clay Dennis was no nine-inning hurler. He surely would need relief before the game

Clothesline Hitter 39

was over. Would Benteen take him out now, before the Bombers got to him, for a pinch hitter?

Lefty watched Art standing out there on second, his arms folded, calmly awaiting the next hitter. Dennis began to peel off his jacket, looking questioningly toward Benteen. The manager stood up.

"Never mind, Clay," he said abruptly. He glanced down the bench and his questing green eyes rested coldly on Lefty. "Hey, you, Tarbin!"

Lefty turned in surprise.

"Get up there an' hit. Bring Gray in. I want that run!"

Just like that. No time to fidget or worry. Just grab a bat, get up there, and hit. Bring in that run!

He felt the sweat trickle down his back. He got up and walked to the bat rack. The piece of lumber he wanted was there. It was a brown-stained, 38-inch Paul Waner model. In practice, Lefty had liked the feel of it. The fat pitches of the throwers had gone screaming off the Waner model like anti-tank rockets. But that was batting practice hurling.

He had the wood in his hand and was standing at the plate. Quietly the Bayville southpaw studied him. The peppy Bomber infield kept up its steady chatter. They shifted slightly toward first base, surmising that Lefty was a pull hitter. A gentle breeze whispered out toward right field, and somewhere in the distance a train whistle echoed loud and long.

The catcher began to needle him. "Well, looka

what we got here. Mama's boy ain't dry behind the ears yet. An' he wants to hit in this-here man's league." The catcher raised his voice. "Aw right, Mel! Knock the bum's ears off!"

Lefty tried not to listen to the catcher. Benteen had said in the clubhouse that Mel Goss liked to get a couple of strikes on the batter with his curve, then whip across a smoke ball for the third strike. Since Lefty was new around here, Goss might try his favorite trick on him right now.

The first one was high and wide, and Lefty watched it go by. Goss was testing him. He could look for the curve now. It came in, headed for the center of the plate, and then broke sharply over the outside corner.

"Stee-rike!" bawled the umpire.

The catcher took a step in front of the plate, got rid of the ball, and growled out of the side of his mouth, "Wassa matter, mama's boy? Yella? 'Fraid to swing?"

Lefty said nothing. The next pitch would either be a waste ball, to get him to bite, or another curve. He guessed that, being a rookie, he'd get the curve again.

It happened that way. The pitch was a carbon copy of the first curve. He stepped into it, swung smoothly, and felt wood collide with horsehide. But he had not judged the speed of the pitch well, and the curve broke before he connected. Instead of going into center field, where he had tried to

Clothesline Hitter 41

dump it, the ball headed for left, curving as it went, and landed three feet foul.

"You was lucky to get a piece of that one," the catcher grumbled through his mask. But there was respect in his voice. He evidently had not expected Lefty to connect at all.

The count was two and two, following another outside pitch. Goss would not want to risk another ball now, since if Lefty did not swing, the following pitch would have to be too good. No, as Benteen had warned, Goss would try to burn the ball past him.

It came in hard to the plate, a little high. Lefty never took his eyes off the ball. The Waner model came around fast. *Crack!* The streak of white flew three feet over the second baseman's head, kept going on a slight rise between center and right field, and nearly went through the high board fence that surrounded the park. Gray easily scored. When the ball got back to the infield, Lefty was on second base.

The small crowd made more noise than had been heard in the Fairmount park all season. It was one of the few chances they ever had to cheer, and they made the most of it. Not for a long time had they seen a ball hit as hard as that. Not by a Beaver, at least.

Lefty died on second when the next batter flied out. He spent the rest of the game on the bench, and yelled like mad with the other Beavers in the last of the eighth when they pushed across another run. But the Bombers tallied twice in the ninth; and despite some master-minding by Benteen in the Beavers' final times at bat, the home team could not score again. Bayville won the game, 3-2.

As the team left the field, Tod Blue put his hand on Lefty's arm. His deep voice held a warm, fatherly note, unlike Benteen's cold rasp. "You'll do, kid," he said. "You stepped into that fast ball like some of these guys go after steak an' French fries. Keep it up."

Behind Tod's smile Lefty saw mirrored the years of hard, driving play and deep baseball lore. For a fleeting moment he wished it were not the fading veteran's job he was after.

"Thanks, Tod," he said. "Thanks a lot." And he meant it.

He was sitting before his locker after showering when Shorty came by.

"Nice goin', Lefty," the trainer said. "I hope you ain't feelin' too cocky, though."

"No, I wouldn't say so, Shorty."

"Swell! Because one thing yuh might as well know, Lefty, right now. Mel Goss will be bearin' down awful hard on you next time!"

Everyone within hearing distance laughed. Lefty understood what Shorty meant. But he didn't care much. He was sure that he could hit any pitcher in the Valley League. Not just Mel Goss. Any of

Clothesline Hitter 43

them. He hoped he'd soon get the chance to prove it.

Meanwhile, in Benteen's cubby-hole of an office, a conference was taking place. Benteen had Tod Blue there and faced his first baseman across the desk. He tapped steadily on the polished surface with a pencil, and there was a purposeful look on his bleak, narrow face.

"I s'pose you can guess why I sent for yuh, Tod."

Blue nodded. "Yeah, sure, Cy. I saw the way Tarbin stayed with Goss an' unloaded on that smoke ball. Honest, Cy, I wouldn't even have seen that ball. My eyes ain't what they used to be."

He paused and sighed. He drew a tired hand across his brow. "Reckon you got the pink slip for me. Can't say as I blame you for lettin' me out."

For once the faintest flicker of a smile moved across Benteen's bleak face. The cold green eyes seemed almost to warm a little. He shook his head slowly and tapped more lightly.

"Not the pink slip, Tod. Not exactly."

Blue looked surprised. "What, then?"

"I want you to stay on as coach, an' make a first baseman out of that green kid. Think yuh can do it?"

Blue chuckled happily. "Think I can do it? He's almost a pro already, Cy. A clothesline hitter like him don't come along every day in the week. But we'll have to work on his fieldin'. I watched him out there before the game today. He ain't a Fancy Dan around that bag. An' when the boys get wise to him, he won't tee off every day like he did out there on Goss. But he's a ball player, Cy. At least, I'll make him one or split a gasket tryin'!"

He hesitated. "How long you aim to keep that kid?"

Benteen slowed his tapping and looked wary.

"Yuh know, Tod, the Beavers have lost a lot of money already this year. The boss has been on my neck plenty. With Tarbin, we'll do better, but we won't break even. To do that, we gotta sell some players. An' the only way to do that is to sell 'em *up*. Up into a major-league chain. See what I mean?"

Tod breathed deeply. "Yeah, I get it, Cy. An' I think you'll be able to sell Tarbin before long. I hope so anyway. I'll do my best."

Benteen's lips came tight across his teeth.

"I hope your best is good enough, Tod. It better be!"

CHAPTER IV

THAT TERRIBLE TARBIN TEMPER

Next day there was no game. Lefty heard nothing about becoming the regular first baseman; but halfway through the long practice session, Tod Blue walked off the bag and said:

"Go ahead, kid. Take over for a while."

He did not have to be told twice.

Coach Chris Myers gave him a rough workout. Myers slammed hard grounders and steaming liners at him relentlessly. Lefty handled nearly all of them cleanly. Repeatedly Myers drilled him in the first-to-second-and-back double play.

Once Lefty tripped getting back to first. Myers made a sarcastic comment, and Lefty's face went crimson. But he tightened his lips, determined not to let his temper cost him his chance with the Beavers.

Batting practice was better fun. Lefty did not face the first-line Fairmount twirlers, of course, but one of the bull-pen brigade, Charlie Oates, seemed anxious to show his stuff. Oates' tantalizing sinker bothered Lefty at first. He kept topping it, hitting slow rollers to the second baseman. Twice he hit nothing but the breeze. Oates grinned broadly.

Tod Blue advised him from behind the cage. "Don't come around so fast. Don't try to murder the ball. Keep your eye on it till it hits the bat. Drop your swing a little on the sinker."

He tried to follow the advice. After two more feeble rollers, he caught the sinker squarely. The ball roared over second base, not a dozen feet off the ground, and hit the left-center fence with a splintering crash. It was one of those clothesline drives that no outfielder could haul down unless he stood directly in its path.

Hugo Matthews cracked, "It'll take half your pay to have that fence mended, if you keep that up!"

Blue took him aside later. "You'll do all right. Just watch the ball from the second it leaves the pitcher's hand. Remember that. Your fieldin'—well, that will come along in time, too. You got a habit of fightin' the ball. Keep on your toes, move fast, but stay loose. That way you can take care of the hard grounders."

A day later the Cole City Blue Sox invaded Beaver Park. The Sox were close on the heels of Bayville, and were determined to narrow the gap in this three-game Beaver series.

It was a boiling June day. Lefty thought, will

That Terrible Tarbin Temper

Tod give out under this blazing sun and give me a chance to play a few innings?

Something better than that was in store for him. Benteen came over just as the Beaver infielders jogged out for their pre-game warm-up. "Get out there, Tarbin!"

At first Lefty did not catch on.

"Take your glove!" Benteen snapped. "You're on first today."

With that, the runty manager turned his back and walked to the end of the bench.

The same old butterflies came back into Lefty's stomach. But he made a fast grab for his mitt and hurried out to the bag. Chris Myers lobbed a practice grounder to third baseman Paul Dubeau. Dubeau scooped it up and threw it with a smooth underarm motion. The ball came floating chest-high into Lefty's glove. It was one of the softest throws he had ever taken.

"Get two!" Myers screamed and hit a daisy cutter to Hugo Matthews at second. Hugo flipped it easily to shortstop Doggy Haines on the bag. Haines shot it bullet-like to first.

There were ten minutes of this, and then the umpire called, "Play ball!" A half-pint Sox athlete walked toward the batter's box, swinging several bludgeons. He tossed two of them away, settled himself at the plate with his club held in a choke grip, and faced Lou Kissell on the mound.

Lefty's stomach kept flip-flopping. He found it hard to believe that he really was installed, for the moment at least, as the Beaver first sacker. The yells and cheers of the fans made a confused, distant murmur. He ran his tongue over dry lips, and punched his left fist into the crab-net glove.

He heard himself yell, "Atta boy, Lou; burn it by him!" Then Kissell's arm flashed down with the opening pitch, and the game was on.

It was a relief that two batters flied to the outfield and the third fanned. Lefty still was in a half-daze, still marvelling that he was holding down first base on a pro club—even a stumbling cellar outfit like the Beavers. Then he was trotting back to the bench, wondering where his name stood in the lineup which Benteen had given to the umpire just before game time.

Benteen called, "Matthews, Haines, Tarbin. C'mon! Shake it up now."

Good! He was batting third, a spot he always had liked.

Matthews tried to beat out a bunt, but was thrown out by Monson, the Blue Sox pitcher. Lefty moved on deck while Doggy Haines batted. Haines crowded the plate. Monson, trying to loosen him up, threw too close and plunked him on the elbow. Grinning and rubbing his arm, Haines eased his way to first.

Lefty knew what was expected of him, even without Benteen's signal. This early in the game, a strong club might have gone for the big inning, but the Beavers always tried to push every possible tally around the safe way. His job was to sacrifice Haines to second.

Monson's first throw was a pitchout. Then the second one came in, big and slow and fat. He did not forget the bunt sign. But the change-up was so inviting, and he was so perfectly set for it, that he could not resist the temptation. He waited till the floater almost reached the plate, and then swung. He caught it squarely on the underside and sent it high and far into the outfield.

As he ran, he could not keep his eyes off the ball. At first he thought it would clear the fence. But it was too high, and came down with a loud crash about two-thirds of the way up the boards. The center fielder played the ball well and held Lefty to a double. Haines had no trouble scoring. Then the shortstop robbed big Red Lynn of a hit with a spectacular running catch of a line drive. Eddie Pinto struck out to retire the side.

Score: Fairmount 1, Cole City 0.

Despite his own failure to score, Lefty was elated as he hustled toward first base for his mitt. To his astonishment, when he got there he found Tod Blue already on the bag. There was a queer look in the veteran's steel-gray eyes.

"Take in your mitt," Tod said, nodding toward the bench. "Benteen wants you."

Amazement rooted Lefty to the ground. For a

moment he could not speak. His face turned beet red as the import of Tod's words and tone sank in.

"You mean—you mean I'm benched?" he finally blurted. "For Pete's sake, why?"

Tod caught a practice throw deftly, tossed a ground ball back across the infield, and said curtly, "Go in there an' find out."

Benteen was waiting. His face was a mask of cold fury.

"Listen, Tarbin," he snarled. "Who yuh think is runnin' this club, you or me? Didn't yuh get that bunt sign?"

"Sure," Lefty said, his indignation rapidly getting the better of his surprise. "But the pitch was in there, and I knew I could hit it. I brought in the run, didn't I?"

The substitutes on the bench sat very quiet. Benteen's voice was coated with hatred. "Now you get this, Tarbin, an' don't forget it, ever! I might excuse a rookie missin' a sign. That could happen. But any so-and-so who deliberately ignores my orders ain't playin' ball for me. If you weren't a rookie, I'd give yuh your walkin' papers right now!"

Something snapped inside Lefty's brain. He hated the guts of this cold, snarling little runt. The two of them would never get along, and it was better that they break up now. Even baseball was not worth trying to tolerate Benteen's kind. The old Tarbin temper flared again, and he flung all reason aside.

That Terrible Tarbin Temper

"The devil with you and your two-bit bunch of stumblebums!" he gritted. "I wouldn't play ball for you again if I starved to death. That's final. I'm through!"

With those words, he stormed into the clubhouse. He brushed past Shorty, who looked surprised but said nothing, and went to his locker. He kicked open the door with a clatter and started undressing. When he was through, he put on his street clothes, not bothering to shower. He slammed the locker door viciously. Putting his shoes and glove in the canvas bag, he rushed out of the building.

At first he intended to catch the evening train out of Fairmount. Then, upon considering, he decided to remain at the hotel overnight. He needed time to plan what to do next. He was through with baseball. That was certain. He'd never play for Benteen or anyone else again. Should he go back to Idaho and confess that his father had been right? Eating humble pie was not Lefty's style, but he thought his dad would welcome him back if he knew Lefty had quit the diamond.

He ate a sandwich before going to his room, because after what had happened he did not want to have supper in the dining hall with the Beavers. When he got upstairs, he stretched out on his bed, still fuming. Art Gray, his roomie, would come in after the game, but he could stand Art. The good-natured outfielder would know how he felt.

It was eight o'clock before anyone arrived. The

team apparently had gone directly to the dining room after the game. This must be Art now, just coming upstairs.

It was Art, all right. But he had two others with him. Tod Blue and Shorty.

"Take it easy," Art said, holding up his hand as his roommate started to come off the bed. "I brought these guys up here. They want to talk to you."

Tod and Shorty said, "Hi." Lefty grunted. He had nothing against the two, but he could not see what they wanted with him.

Shorty cleared his throat. "Lefty," he said almost sadly, "I finally seen what the grapevine meant about the Tarbin temper."

"So you heard. Well, what about it?"

"Seems like the temper sometimes runs the other Tarbin parts."

Lefty started to growl something, but he liked Shorty, so he cut it off.

Tod said quietly, "What Shorty means is that we all hate to see you throw away a shot at the big leagues because of what happened out there today."

"The big leagues!" Lefty snorted. "The way things are run in this game, I'd be lucky to get out of this hick Valley League. No, sir. I'm through!"

Shorty said, "I knew a guy once—an' I've heerd of a half dozen more—right up in the majors, who did what you did today. They just couldn't let the

That Terrible Tarbin Temper

fat pitch go by. They didn't want to bunt. Three of 'em smacked the ball out of the park, too. But they got benched just the same."

Lefty was interested, though he tried to hide the fact. "What else happened to them?"

"They was blasted by their managers, like you was. But every one of 'em had the guts to go back in there and play the game right."

Lefty came off the bed, pounding one fist into the other. He paced the room. He had never thought that anyone would react as Shorty said the major leaguers did, after being bawled out by their managers for doing something they thought was all right.

Tod saw the opening they had made. "Looka here, kid. I happen to know that Benteen, no matter what he said today, thinks you're one of the best prospects ever to come intuh this league. He's as disappointed as you are about what happened. But he knows you were wrong. You shoulda followed orders. An' he *can't* back down. If he did, club discipline would fall apart. Can't you see his side of it?"

"No," Lefty growled. "I can't. I brought in that run for Benteen, and I might have scored another one. That's what the Beavers need, isn't it—runs?"

Tod was patient. "We need runs all right," he said grimly. "We lost the game today, two to one. Maybe you didn't know."

"Let's go," Shorty interrupted. "Lefty can make up his own mind. Whether he's a ball player or a quitter."

He turned on his heel and went out the door. Tod followed him.

Lefty paced the room for several minutes, thinking hard. Bobby Dale's words came back to him, out of the past. *You've got to control that temper of yours. It's your worst enemy!*

Maybe Bobby was right. Maybe today he had flown off the handle too fast. Too fast for his own good, anyway. Slowly he turned to Art, who slouched apparently unconcerned in the easy chair. "What do you think, Art?"

The outfielder studied his fingernails for a moment. Then he said, "Lefty, I sure wish I could swing that lumber like you can. If I could, there wouldn't be a thrower in baseball who could keep me outta the big time."

"You mean that?"

Art nodded. "The way I see it, you can't miss. And I got a hunch Benteen and Tod think so, too. Else Shorty and Tod never would have come up here tonight."

Lefty continued to pace the floor. He was torn between his love for baseball and his still hot anger against Benteen. Finally he sat down and said, "What you think I should do?"

His friend came slowly out of his chair. "I bet if

That Terrible Tarbin Temper 55

you talk to Benteen in the morning and admit you were wrong, he'll take you back."

"We-e-ll." Lefty hesitated. "I don't know."

Art grabbed his advantage. "In the morning we'll see Benteen. Okay?"

"Well—okay."

The first person they saw next morning was Tod. The veteran readily agreed to go with Lefty to Benteen and try to patch things up.

Lefty was surprised at Benteen's indifference. He seemed entirely to have forgotten yesterday's quarrel. "Sure, kid," he said, his green eyes as bleak as ever. "No apologies needed. Long as you agree to follow the signs you get on the field, the Beavers sure can use yuh."

That afternoon Lefty broke up a 2-2 tie game with the Blue Sox by socking a fast ball over the right field fence.

It's great to be a ball player. Even with the Fairmount Beavers!

That was a long, hot summer. By the Fourth of July, the Beavers, sparked by Lefty's smoking bat and improved play in the field, had the fans streaming back to the park. Art Gray, getting into more and more games in center field, became a better hitter with Lefty's help. The two often went out to the field in the morning for extra practice.

Tod Blue smiled quietly on the first-base coaching lines, encouraging Lefty, helping him with precious hints on first-base play. Benteen remained as cold and tight-lipped as ever, but there was a pleased light in his fathomless green eyes as he watched Lefty's steady improvement.

The Beavers played a double-header at home with Bluefield on Labor Day. Bluefield held fourth place in the league, with Fairmount, at last out of the cellar, only one game behind in the fifth spot. If the Beavers could win both games that day, they would climb into fourth. While that was as high as they could hope to go, with only ten days of the season left, it was far better than what most fans had hoped for in May.

Fairmount won the opener, 4-3, on a long double by Red Lynn with Doggy Haines on third. The second contest dragged into late innings without a score. Lou Kissell was pitching tightly against Socks Adams of the Bluefields.

"If yuh get on base, run like the devil is after you," Benteen told his players.

In the last of the eighth Lefty came to bat with two out. He had a pair of hits in the first game, and a single in the second. Now the pitcher threw more cautiously. Lefty hit a long foul to left; then Adams, evidently afraid to let him hit, threw four straight balls.

Lefty's mind raced as he jogged toward first. Watching Adams from the corner of his eye, he saw him face toward third base and reach for dirt to rub over the ball. That was all Lefty needed.

That Terrible Tarbin Temper

Pretending to halt on first base, he suddenly let loose a burst of speed and rounded the bag toward second.

Adams, not noticing Lefty's break for second, continued his casual rubbing of the ball. Frantic yells of his teammates finally roused him, and he whirled in surprise. By this time Lefty, dirt spouting under flying spikes, was two-thirds of the way to second. Bluefield's keystone sacker raced him to the bag.

Adams' hurried throw came in fast, on the far side. Lefty took off in a long hook slide that carried him hard into the second baseman. The latter got his hands on the ball, but by the time he made the tag, Lefty's foot was in there.

A roaring crescendo of sound poured from the stands. Every Beaver rooter was out of his seat, cheering like mad. A player taking second on a base on balls! It was a daring play which they often had read about; but never before had they actually seen it tried. As Lefty rose to his feet, brushing dirt from his pants, the dust rose about him in a slow-moving cloud. The gritty taste of it bit into his throat and made him cough.

Clean-up hitter Red Lynn, whose double won the first game, walked to the plate. Adams betrayed his nervousness out there on the mound. The count ran to three and two, and Lynn watched the next pitch go by. It was the fourth ball, and Red took his base.

Art Gray, batting next, hit the first pitch into center field for a single. Lefty, pounding home to beat the throw, slid under the catcher and watched the umpire's palms go down in the safe sign.

That ended the scoring. In the first of the ninth, Bluefield went down one-two-three, and the Beavers had the ball game and fourth place.

The Beavers were scheduled to finish the season on the road, leaving Fairmount next morning on the team's bus. Benteen met Lefty and Art in the hotel elevator that evening while they were on their way upstairs. He asked them to come to his room.

Lefty, despite his fine headwork of the afternoon, felt uneasy as they followed the manager along the carpetless corridor. He thought that Art, though more easy-going, must feel the same way. Yet when Lefty glanced at him, the blonde outfielder merely shrugged and lifted his eyebrows.

Benteen motioned them into the room and shut the door. He put his hat in the closet, threw a copy of the *Clarion* on the bed, and pointed to some chairs. His face was as emotionless as ever.

What was this all about?

Benteen sat down on the only remaining chair and crossed his legs. He came to the point directly.

"Got news for yuh," he said. "You both been aimin' to stay in baseball, I s'pose?"

They nodded. Was he going to be fatherly and advise them to get into something else while they were still young enough?

That Terrible Tarbin Temper

"Well," Benteen continued, "then maybe you will think it's good news. Both of you have been sold to the Detroit Tigers. You report next spring for trainin' with their Blue River team in the Midland League. That's a class A ball club."

For a moment they sat there, stunned. Art was the first to break the silence. He yelled, *"Yippee—ee!"*

Lefty jumped to his feet a split second before Art did. He never remembered what he shouted. It did not matter. The two of them, arms around each other, were dancing about the room. Then Art broke away and did an Indian war dance by himself. Lefty followed suit.

The last look Lefty had of him, Benteen was rubbing his chin and smiling broadly. At least for Benteen it was a broad smile; and some of it even was reflected in the usually cold green eyes.

They yelled, "Thanks, Mr. Benteen!" over their shoulders and went singing down the corridor.

When they got to their room, they finished the celebration with a pillow fight.

CHAPTER V

WINTER IN FLORIDA

Lefty finished the Beaver season on a cloud of happiness. When the team arrived back at Fairmount ten days later, just before disbanding for the year, he found that he had batted .319 in seventy-five games and had hit ten homers, three triples, and nineteen doubles.

"No wonder the Tigers bought you," Shorty cackled across the locker room. "A long ball hitter with an average like that is goin' to look mighty good some day in Briggs Stadium!"

"If I ever get there," Lefty cautioned.

"You'll get there, all right. That is, if you can control that temper of yours. Some people are already callin' you an umpire baiter."

"I don't bait 'em. I only stand up for my rights."

Shorty changed the subject. "What you doin' till spring trainin' starts?"

Lefty shook his head. "I don't know. Thought I might go home for a visit. But I told you how my dad feels about baseball. And I haven't saved much on this year's salary."

"Yeah, I know," Shorty grunted. "Your dad's attitude is sure strange. Say, look. You don't wanna go home an' ask yore old man for a winter job. I can see that. Why don't you go to Florida now, an' work until the Blue River trainin' camp opens in March?"

"And what would I use for money?"

The trainer winked. "That's where yore ol' Uncle Shorty comes in. He knows every hotel owner and manager on the West Florida coast. Known 'em since I played ball down there myself about—well, quite a few years ago. If I can't get you a job as desk clerk, elevator boy, or soda jerk, I'll eat this-here rubbin' table!"

"Wouldn't wanna swallow a meal like that," someone drawled. It was Art Gray, who had just come into the room. "Did I hear you say something about a job, Shorty? A real, money-paying job?"

"Yuh heerd right. I'm gettin' Lefty a job in Florida, for the winter."

"I need a job, too. How about me?"

"Well, why don't the two of yuh go down there right now, together? With my recommendation—"

"They'll both starve," chirped a voice along the bench.

"—they'll both be fit an' rarin' to go when spring rolls 'round," Shorty finished positively.

So it was that the two Tiger hopefuls found themselves riding the Florida special one day early in October. They had come by way of New York, to see the closing games of the World's Series.

"Those guys sure were born to play baseball," Art enthused, referring to the members of the championship teams.

Lefty smiled in agreement. "If either of us turns out to be as good as they are, we ought to be up there, too, in time."

The train sped along in sight of distant Virginia blue ridges. Art's face took on a thoughtful cast.

"You've told me your father hates baseball," he said. "I know how you must feel. But I guess I've never mentioned that I want to prove something to my dad, too, by making good in the majors. You see, Dad had a cup of coffee with the Athletics years ago, but didn't make the grade. He was an outfielder, too. Now his hopes are all bound up in me. He wants to see me play in the big leagues, where he failed. My problem is a little different from yours, but the pressure is there just the same."

Lefty gazed at the distant blue ridges. The slanting, late afternoon sun shone bright on the far-off hills. He could not say anything in answer to Art's tale of a father's frustrated hope, born again in a son who had the makings of a major leaguer. He just stared at the soft blue slopes and wished that he were fighting for a place in the big show because his father wanted it that way.

Shorty had given them the names of a dozen hotel men on Florida's West Coast. When they arrived there, they spent two days on the beaches, and then started making the hotel rounds in Tampa.

The first three managers they saw knew Shorty, and were glad to meet the trainer's friends. But at

Winter in Florida

the moment there were no jobs open. The third one, though, had a suggestion.

"Old Pete Travers—he was one of Shorty's ball-player pals—manages a place in Sarasota. That's only twenty-five miles from Galesville, where the Tigers' Blue River farm team trains. Maybe Pete could use you. He has more of a turnover in help than we do."

So they took a bus to Sarasota and found the Vista Hotel. The man behind the desk turned out to be Pete Travers himself. He welcomed them like long-lost brothers.

"If you're pals of that-there broken-down infielder, Shorty Timmins," Pete rumbled, "you're sure welcome here. An' if it's jobs yuh want, the welcome goes double. I'm on this-here desk because the reg'lar clerk is runnin' the elevator. I need two husky lads to double up on the elevator an' baggage-carryin', an' if you'll stay, you're life savers. There's room for both of yuh to sleep here, too."

They took the jobs.

At first Lefty thought that running an elevator would not be active enough to keep him in shape all winter. He had a tendency to put on weight, and his six-feet-two easily could carry far more than two hundred pounds. But he wanted to tip the scales at an even two hundred in March. This would leave him ten pounds to take off in training, and he could start league play at his usual one-ninety.

That was *if* he made the Blue River team!

Neither he nor Art, it turned out, needed to worry about putting on weight. Their jobs were not soft. They stayed on their feet twelve hours a day, carrying guests' luggage, acting as bell hops, and in general filling the roles of muscular handymen. Every evening found them dog-tired.

"In Fairmount I used to sleep like a log," Art said. "Here a sleeping log would look like a victim of St. Vitus dance, compared to me when I hit the hay."

Partridge hunting in the hills of New England couldn't have put more spring in their legs. The fresh salt air and steady exercise did more to keep them in shape than they could have done for themselves by seeking exercise through play.

"This is the fastest winter I've ever spent," Lefty said as the weeks and months flew by.

"Me too," Art agreed. "And one of the nicest. We don't get much time to ourselves, but when we do —the salt water and the palm trees sure are wonderful!"

Christmas came and passed, with gifts exchanged with home folks by mail. Lefty's father made no direct reference to ball playing, but wrote that he was glad Lefty was making his way on his own.

For the two ball players, February seemed like the very beginning of a new year. It was then that little items of baseball news began creeping into the papers. Some major leaguers were signing con-

Winter in Florida

tracts; others threatened to hold out for higher salaries. The Dodgers hired a new manager, and up in Cleveland the Indians were confident that this was to be their year.

Suddenly one morning at breakfast, Lefty—who had been reading as he ate—touched Art's arm. He had just seen an item in Gus Kirke's "Sports Parade" column.

"The Class A Blue River Eagles," Gus wrote, "will train again this year at Galesville. That Galesville ball park (can we call it one?) is a horror. But last year, so were the Eagles. This season it's going to be different. Manager Whitey Whelan says so. He has a flock of whiz kids who'll put Blue River back in its proper baseball channel . . . Maybe . . . They do say, though, that two kids from class C ball might have the goods. They are Lefty Tarbin, a first baseman who hits 'em a mile, and Art Gray, the lad who some day will make big league fans forget the likes of Speaker, Cobb, DiMaggio. We'll believe that when we see it."

They enjoyed the item, and showed it to Pete. He liked it, too.

"They'll have lots of fun with you kids," he said. "But don't let that bother yuh. For a while they called Shorty Timmins the 'Tallahassee Turtle,' when we trained there years ago. But that little round guy sure could play third base. Them writers was singin' another tune mighty quick."

They were due to report at the main Tiger camp

in Lakeview on the first of March, and then go to Galesville for the Blue River opening of training on the fifteenth. One afternoon, a few days before they were to leave Vista Hotel, they had a breathing spell and were sitting in their room, waiting to jump if Pete rang. There was a knock on the door, and when they yelled "Coming!"—thinking it was Pete—the door opened and a light-haired man of about forty-five walked in. He was of medium build, with wide shoulders and an easy carriage. He looked capable.

"You're Tarbin and Gray," he immediately stated rather than asked. He flashed a quick, easy smile as he stuck out his hand. "I'm Whitey Whelan, your new manager."

Whelan obviously was an entirely different type from Benteen. He put the two athletes at ease right away. "I'll be in Sarasota for several days on business. If you fellows are ready when I leave, I'll drive you to Lakeview. That way we can get acquainted faster. Okay?"

Of course they were delighted. Not since prep school days had Lefty known a coach or manager to whom he had warmed up at all. Every one of them had been either, like Coach Carey at Bolton, indifferent, or like Benteen, openly hostile. Maybe it had been the Tarbin temper that was responsible. Well, if this man Whelan was as pleasant as he appeared, Lefty would try to see that his own hot temper did not spoil their good relations.

Winter in Florida

They said good-bye and thanks to Pete a few days later and climbed into Whelan's convertible. It was a beautiful afternoon, full of Florida sunshine. Whelan drove leisurely, and during the trip he did most of the talking. Apparently there were things about the Eagles set-up that he wanted them to know.

"Gray, we'll have ten outfielders in camp, and we're keeping five of them. But you shouldn't have much trouble hanging on, because three are definitely set for one of our class B teams, and two others may go lower than that. Benteen is sure you'll stick, and I think so too. I've seen you play."

The road was a smooth ribbon of concrete before them.

"Your case, Tarbin, is a little different. Right now you're the only first baseman we have, unless we convert one of the outfielders. Last year's regular first baseman, Tom Silk, has moved up to double-A Manchester this year in the Tiger chain. If he makes it there, you're in at Blue River. Tom isn't much of a fielder. He'll improve, but the big brass may think he needs another year in class A. If so, you'll have competition on your hands. Silk is a real hitter."

All this was news to Lefty; but, he reflected, it was better than he had expected. Even if the old Eagle first sacker came back, there would be a fight for the job. And if his own hitting held up, he could at least hope for a place as a pinch hitter.

Reaching Lakeview, they drove past the ball park en route to the hotel. The place was surrounded by a high board fence, and the top of the stands showed above the fence. It did not look any more impressive from the outside than did the Fairmount park. But no doubt it filled the bill for spring training.

The city turned out to be crowded with players in the Detroit chain. Tiger chiefs wanted a look at all their baseball ivory; so through the organization's Lakeview training camp passed every one of their hired hands at or above class C level.

Everything, Lefty discovered, went by clockwork routine. They reported on the big field at ten o'clock on the morning of March first, and from then until three in the afternoon every minute of every player's time was accounted for. The first few days involved loosening up and easy throwing. Then it was fielding drill for so many minutes, batting practice that gave each hitter just so many swings, and sliding, bunting, and tagging workouts aimed at nothing less than perfection in those skills. The first basemen spent hours with the pitchers, working on the play where the pitcher covered first base while the baseman fielded the ball.

Lefty had never seen anything handled with such smooth precision. This business of trying for a spot in a major league system really was something!

One thing puzzled him, as it did Art. No one seemed to be paying any attention to them individ-

Winter in Florida 69

ually. They had their schedule of assigned workouts, and followed them faithfully. But Whitey Whelan, though he was on the field in uniform every day, hardly ever spoke to either of them. He seemed always in conference with two or three other field managers or Tiger officials.

Once, however, Lefty found that someone's eyes were on him. He disliked sliding practice, and one afternoon he stalled for a few minutes before going over to the sliding pit.

"Hey, Tarbin, get goin'!" a voice rasped across the field. "If there's one thing you need, it's a workout in that pit."

He never tried to dodge work again. "I'm going to get that first base job if I have to scrape the skin off my legs clear down to both ankles," he told Art grimly.

Presently he got a look at his possible rival, Tom Silk, who also stopped over at Lakeview before going on to the Manchester camp. Silk was a big, rugged man, weighing over two hundred pounds, who hit a long ball and hit it hard. But he was far from a Fancy Dan at first base. If he came back to the Eagles, Lefty felt sure he could field better than Silk did and bat on nearly equal terms.

Mid-March came roaring on while this daily routine continued. Players trickled out of camp every day. Finally it was time for the Eagles group to leave, and they set out in a bus for Galesville.

The Galesville field, twenty-five miles down the

coast, was nearly as good as the one at Lakeview. The playing surface appeared in good condition, the grass close-cropped and the infield wide and smooth. Probably Gus Kirke's jibes in his column about the field had jolted the owners into action.

"Anyone who can't show his stuff on this diamond," Lefty thought as he stepped out on it next day, "won't show it anywhere."

Whelan confined the morning's workout to fielding and batting drill. In the afternoon he called for a three-inning practice game. In the A lineup, Lefty was on first base. Art patrolled center field for the B team, with a spare outfielder filling in at first base for the B's.

The varsity infield looked speedy. Lefty, thanks to Tod Blue's patient coaching, knew he now was at least a passable glove man. He was confident that he would hit well. At second base, an eighteen-year-old kid named Jay Titus played with the confidence and effortless ease of an older man. Shortstop Tuck Hanson was a veteran a little past his prime, but still plenty fast. From the hot corner Jackie Kent rifled throws to Lefty that hit the bull's eye every time.

On Lefty's first trip to the plate in the short contest, he boomed one of his patented clothesline drives to the right of center. It looked like an easy double; but Art, moving like a greyhound, managed to haul it down. Next time, he singled to left on a fast curve. He swung late, and knew that he

Winter in Florida

needed more practice in getting his bat around faster.

He pretended to be angry with Art for the fleet center fielder's catch of his line drive.

"I'll get even with you," he promised as they passed on the field between innings. "You robber!"

When Art came to bat his second time, after singling his first trip, Lefty had a chance to make good his threat. A B runner was on first, and Lefty guessed that the hit-and-run was on.

He was right. The base runner moved for second on the pitch and Art hit into the hole behind him. Jay Titus had moved to cover second. It was Lefty's ball or a base hit.

He lunged desperately for the skidding horsehide, flung out his gloved right hand as the pellet kicked up dust on the basepath. The crab-net went into the dirt like a scoop. When Lefty brought the glove up, he was not sure whether the ball was in there.

The base runner already was sliding into second. Too late to get him. There was not time either to look in the glove for the ball or to make the turn back toward first. He stuck his left hand quickly into the pocket of the mitt, and the ball was there. In the same motion, his back still toward first base, he flipped a back-hand throw.

Here was where the endless hours of practice at Lakeview paid off. The pitcher had run to cover first as soon as Art hit the ball. Lefty's back-hand toss travelled a little to the home plate side of the bag, and the running hurler plucked it out of the air just as he crossed the sack. Art was out by a step.

Art grinned ruefully as Lefty walked back.

"We're all even now, you holdup man!" he said. Then, as he moved away, he called over his shoulder, "That was really a honey. You can play on my team any day."

That was how things moved in the remaining weeks of practice. There were only a few veterans holding over from last year's team, but the youngsters fitted into the lineup like parts of a jig-saw puzzle. By the time the season was ready to begin in April, Art was first string in center field, and the Eagles were being referred to in the sports pages as "Whelan's Whizzes." It looked as if the whiz kids really were going to make Blue River forget about the previous year's misfit club.

Whelan took his charges on the long trip over the road in a bus from Galesville to the home park at Blue River. There were two days of workouts on the Eagle field, and Whelan made the last one an easy morning affair. He told the players to relax until game time next day.

The Eagles opened at home against the Blackstone Reds. The Reds had won the pennant the year before in the eight-team Midland League. Could the whiz kids, or anyone else, stop them from doing it again?

CHAPTER VI

TOM SILK RETURNS

OPENING day broke cool and clear, the answer to everyone's hopes. Both teams came out on the field more than an hour before two o'clock game time.

"Look at those stands!" Art said. "They're packed. Must be at least ten thousand people here."

Tuck Hanson hitched at his belt as he took part in the pepper game. "Plenty of 'em up there now; but to keep 'em there, we gotta play ball. Real ball, all year."

Lefty knew what Tuck meant. He remembered how the fans streamed into the park at Fairmount when the team won, and stayed home during a losing streak.

The march to the outfield flagpole, and the raising of the Stars and Stripes, were soon over. The teams ran through their pregame workouts, and then the Eagles took the field for the few minutes before the umpire's cry of "Play ball!"

Opening game nervousness hit Lefty again, just as always. Whenever a new season began, and he stood out there waiting for the opening pitch, the first crack of bat against ball, his palms grew moist and his knees weak. Then, when the game at last was on, he was relaxed and easy again. It was nothing more than the natural stage fright that comes even to veteran performers.

Quickly he surveyed the Eagle infield. Young but confident Jay Titus, loose Tuck Hanson, and steady Jackie Kent. He glanced swiftly too at the outfield, and was glad to see Art out there, lithe and poised as a greyhound. If ever a ball club had possibilities, it was this Eagles bunch.

The batter swung hard at an outside curve. He topped the ball, coming around late, and it skidded close to the ground toward Jay. Jay kneeled down, trapped the sphere with his glove, and threw out the runner.

The fans could tell the difference, the way the ball was snapped around the infield after the put-out. There was confidence and poise in the lively chatter of the players.

This is the kind of pepper that carries a club to the pennant!

The Reds went out one-two-three in that inning. In the Eagles half, Jay led off. He worked the count to three and two, and then drew a pass.

Art Gray came out of the circle. He could hit behind the runner, bunt, and go down to first base with the fastest of them. Whelan had him batting second. This time, it being early in the game, Whelan flashed him the hit sign from the bench.

Art hit the ball hard, but on the ground. The

Tom Silk Returns

Red second sacker took the grounder and pegged to the shortstop on second. Jay slid in high and fast. He was out, but he hurried the throw to first, and it sailed over the first baseman's head into the Eagle dugout. Art kept going until he reached second base.

Frank Church, right fielder, came up next. Frank hit two long fouls, and the left fielder caught the second one. Two out, and Lefty's turn at bat. He had not expected to bat clean-up. Church and the left fielder, Elmer Flagg, were power hitters and either might have had the fourth spot.

"But I think you're steadier than Church or Flagg," Whelan had said. "Lots of doubles with men on base can be more help to us than occasional home runs."

So now, Lefty was aware, Whelan would gladly settle for a clothesline double. A single, for that matter, would bring in the run.

The first pitch came down the middle. Too eager, he swung early and pulled the ball outside first base. The crafty Red hurler next gave him two balls, but he refused to bite at either of them.

Then the right pitch came in. It was high and away from the batter, but definitely in the strike zone. At first he considered letting it go by. From the back of his mind, however, he remembered Tod Blue's advice: "Never let a strike go by in hopes of gettin' something better. Those guys just don't pitch you that way."

So he decided to forget about the fences this time. He poked with the bat and dunked the ball safely into short right center, a blooper hit. By the time the Red outfielder got the ball, Art was crossing the plate and Lefty stood on first base.

Later, he thanked his lucky stars for using good judgment. Because that run was the only score of the contest, winning it for the Eagles.

Whitey Whelan was happy over the game, and for more than simply the fact that his team won it.

"My boys played real ball," he told the baseball writers proudly. "I've got three green kids in the infield, but Tuck Hanson will hold them together. Wait an' see. The outfield could be faster on the flanks, but did you ever see anybody run like that kid Gray in center? He'll cover more ground than a centipede. If his hitting only holds up!"

The smile grew wider on Whitey's genial face. "That boy Tarbin won the game for us with his bat. And his fielding—well, he's no Hal Chase yet, but give him time. Yes sir, you don't recognize the old Eagles, do you? They're one hundred per cent better than last year!"

Through the days and weeks that followed, Whitey's prediction grew to look better and better. After a month of play, the team was in second place, close on the heels of the champion Reds. When the searing dog-days of August came, the Red veterans—too old now for a full, scorching season of tough play—would fold. At least, that was what Whitey promised.

"You betcha life them guys will fold," Tuck grinned. "Me, I know. My legs feel it more every year. But with these whiz kids aroun' me, I should get by one more season."

These were happy days for Lefty. He was batting over three hundred, he had made only a few errors, and as yet had quarrelled violently with exactly no one. That furious Tarbin temper was in check, it appeared, and Lefty was beginning to love even the umpires. That is the way it is when a team is winning.

Nevertheless, the Eagles did not plod along entirely peacefully. They did plenty of screaming and clawing. Catcher Cass Melrose jawed incessantly at enemy batters. At short, Tuck was a real holler guy. Lefty himself went all out every minute, and on the base paths as a runner he tried to use some of the tricks Ty Cobb had made famous.

One day he slid with a bang into the opposing second baseman. He saw that he was certain to be tagged out. But, hoping to break up a double play, he flung himself as hard as he could into the bag. The double play collapsed, all right, but he also accidentally spiked the infielder. This player drew back his fist to slug Lefty, when the umpire Hogan stepped between them.

Lefty grinned as he entered the dugout.

"I haven't fought anybody yet," he said. "But Hogan sure saved my record today. If that guy had hit me, I guess this time I'd have blown my top."

Good things cannot go on forever. Lefty discovered the truth of this the hard way. He was dressing for the Memorial Day doubleheader when a burly, familiar figure swaggered into the clubhouse. His heart did a loop-the-loop when he saw the man. It was Tom Silk. He could have come back for only one reason.

"Nope, I didn't make it up there," Silk admitted. "Not this time. Guess I ain't ready for double-A yet. Shucks, I'll be back there again, you bet; but for this season yuh can bank on me to win that old pennant for the Eagles."

Lefty's face flushed with resentment and he kept his eyes down on his locker. He knew the rest of the team, silent now, were sending curious glances in his direction. He had been playing good ball so far. But at times, he knew, his inexperience in this faster company showed up. Could he compete successfully against the hitting power and greater baseball savvy of the demoted veteran from Manchester?

It was to be a nip-and-tuck struggle for some days. Silk did not get into the regular lineup immediately. But in the second half of that same Memorial Day doubleheader, with the score tied in the ninth, Whelan yanked his pitcher and sent the hard-hitting Silk to the plate.

The Manchester castoff repaid Whitey's confidence by smashing the ball over the right field fence. The long blow won the game, and it became apparent that Silk would have to be put in the lineup somewhere. The team was winning, however, and no manager likes to break up a successful combination. So for a while Lefty held onto his job.

Two weeks later the Eagles' luck began to change, as it was bound to do. The team lost three games in a row. And as bad luck would have it, Lefty went hitless in all three of them. In the last one, he got into a jam with the first-base umpire and later was the center of a heated rhubarb with several players of the Oaktown club after some rough action around first base.

Before the game next day Whitey took him aside.

"Look, kid," he said kindly. "I know you're playin' your heart out, an' I know there's more than one reason for it. You're a good team man, and a fighter. But your nerves are on edge. You need a rest. I'm puttin' Silk out there today."

Tears nearly came to Lefty's eyes. He almost flung a sharp, bitter retort in Whitey's face. Even though the blow was not unexpected, his disappointment was hardly lessened. But partly out of respect for the manager, and partly because of his firm resolution to keep out of trouble, he closed his mouth and sat quietly, though disconsolately, on the bench.

What he saw in the following days did not make

him feel any better. Silk was a terrific hitter, no doubt of that. He had more power, if less consistency, than Lefty did. Runners moved farther on Tom's drives, a good proportion of which sailed out of the park or against the far barriers. The crowd loved it, the Eagles began to win again, and attendance picked up.

Art tried to cheer up Lefty. "You'll be back in there soon. Silk's got more power, sure. But you'll always hit for a better average. Whitey knows that as well as we do. An' if Silk can ever come anywhere near you as a fielder, I'll make a sandwich outta his glove an' eat it, raw!"

Lefty smiled tightly. "You may have to eat it, then. Tom's doing all right around that bag, far as I can see."

With the Eagles back on the winning path, Silk appeared more certain of first base than ever. Lefty pinch batted every few days, and in that job he clouted the ball for over four hundred. Such a performance, Whelan naturally figured, made Lefty more valuable as a pinch hitter. That was all right, but Lefty wanted to be in the regular lineup.

Then Fate came back on his side. Or so it seemed at first. In the second inning of a game with the Cairo Bisons late in June, Silk got a deep spike wound in his ankle when a Bison slid back into first base to avoid a pick-off throw. Whitey had to take the veteran out of the game.

"Get out there, Lefty," Whitey said.

Tom Silk Returns

He did not have to speak twice. Lefty grabbed his crab-net and ran onto the field. As the game moved along, he felt better and better. He dug several low throws out of the dirt with a skill that he knew Silk never could have shown. He thought he sensed a confidence in him among the rest of the infield that was not there when Silk fielded the bag. But the other infielders kept mum about it.

At the plate he did not do as well. In his first three times he flied out twice, and the third time, with the game scoreless and Jay on second, he struck out.

"I'll get a hit this time or break my neck trying," he promised himself on his fourth trip. It was the last of the eighth, two outs, and no score had been made as yet by either team.

The Bison moundsman fooled him badly on the very first pitch. Lefty swung at a crazy-breaking screwball, and missed it by nearly a foot. Grinning, the pitcher teased him with a slow ball. He let that go by, too high for a strike.

"Why didn't ya swing?" needled the catcher. "A bad ball will go just as far as a good one—if ya hit it!"

Lefty refused to let that kind of talk get his goat. He knew the next pitch would have to be fast, and probably a strike. It would be either high and close, or a sharp-breaking curve. That was all this particular Bison had. Then the guy would waste one, and try next to get him on another screwball.

He closed his lips tightly. He had no intention of letting their strategy develop that far.

The pitch came as he expected. It zoomed for the plate like a rocket. Would it be merely a straight fast ball, or a curve? Lefty did not intend to wait and see. As the ball roared in, he hitched himself forward, swung his bat, and got the fat of the wood on the pitch as it came over the plate.

The result was another bullet-like clothesline drive. Lefty knew he was back in his batting groove before he completed the swing. The hard-hit ball travelled over the outfield on a line, rising slightly, and looking for a moment as though it would clear the fence. But it hit several feet from the top, the impact sounding like a rifle shot, and bounded back onto the field.

Meanwhile Lefty was pounding toward first. He circled the bag without slowing and headed for second. He saw the ball rebound toward center field, saw the Bison gardener play it cleverly off the wall. The race to second would be close, but he had made it safely many times before, and had no doubt that this time he would beat the fielder's throw again.

The white sphere flew toward the infield, hit the grass, and bounced straight for the waiting Bison on second. The play would be closer than he thought. Too close for comfort.

He went flying through the air. His right leg stayed high, the left bent underneath it to hook the bag as he came in. The left foot caught the bag and he twisted to pull himself away from the infielder, who was just whirling to touch him out. He was safe by an eyelash.

Many times he had made the play, in precisely the same manner. Each time before, he remembered looking up through the hanging dust cloud, eyes squinting, to catch the umpire's sign. But today it was different. The play was somehow not the same. Something went wrong.

As his left foot hooked the base and he tried to twist away, the leg somehow caught. He heard something snap, felt agonizing pain race up his leg. He knew he was safe. Yet he could not look up at the umpire. He moaned, pain-ridden, in the settling dust beside the bag.

They carried him off the field, his left leg bent at a weird angle. He felt himself being lowered onto the rubbing table in the dressing room, inhaled the acrid smell of liniment, heard the low, worried tones of those about him.

He gritted his teeth and opened tear-stained eyes. Doc Herbert and the trainer bent over him. The doctor nodded at the unspoken question in Lefty's hazel eyes. It was a question no one needed to ask.

"Sorry, kid," the doc said. "It's broken. Broken bad. You won't play ball again this season. If ever!"

CHAPTER VII

HOME, SWEET HOME, IN IDAHO

In the days that followed, as Lefty fretted and fussed on the hospital bed, the whole world seemed dark as Cy Benteen's ugliest scowl. He had plenty of visitors, fans and players alike, but none cheered him up much. What he wanted more than anything else was to get on his feet and play ball again.

There was one ray of light that came through the gloom. His injury was not quite as bad as Doc Herbert had feared.

"You'll be on crutches in three weeks," the doc said. "In five or six weeks you can throw the crutches away. But you'll have to take it easy on that foot."

Five or six weeks! That would make it after the first of August. And he would still be limping.

The doctor shook his head in answer to what

Home, Sweet Home, in Idaho

Lefty was thinking. "Better not try to play any more baseball this year. You're young, and the break should heal fast. My advice, though, is to give the leg a good, long rest."

Whitey firmly backed up the doctor's opinion.

"We want you in good shape next spring. Silk is back in the lineup again, an' since you would have to favor that leg, you'd never chase him off the bag this year. But," Whitey grinned encouragingly, "maybe you'll run him outta the league next year!"

So it was decided. Lefty wrote a long letter home, explaining the situation. He would be in no need of money, as his Eagles salary would continue in full all season. He was definitely not coming home a failure. He just wanted to pay an overdue visit.

His father did not wait to write a letter. He telegraphed: "Come home as soon as possible. Can't wait to see you."

A week after the cast was off his leg, he boarded a train for the West Coast. The Eagles were playing that day, still fighting for the pennant, but Whitey and most of the boys came to see him off on the early morning express.

It was a long, tiring ride, especially after he switched trains at Chicago. Chiefly on his mind, besides thoughts of next season, was the question: How will Dad receive me? He knew that Tarbin senior would still be a confirmed baseball hater. The older man did not change his opinions readily.

But perhaps if the subject was not mentioned, no arguments would come up.

At San Francisco he bought a ticket for Seattle, where another rail journey would carry him to Indian Gap, Idaho—his home town. It was a roundabout way, but he wanted to see one or two Pacific Coast League baseball games. A stop-over of a day in San Francisco, and maybe another day in Seattle, where the Rainiers played, would give him an idea of what Coast League ball was like. Maybe some day he would be playing in that classification.

At the parks in both cities he saw plenty of good baseball. The Coast League, he reflected, was almost as fast as the majors. It was from this circuit that many players made the final jump to the big time.

"Art Gray could play ball here," he mused. "So could Jackie Kent. And I'll bet I could too!"

When the local train pulled into Indian Gap, he felt a lot better. Next year he would resume the arduous climb up the baseball ladder. Even if he had to stop off for a while in every league in organized ball, he would never be satisfied until his name appeared on a big league roster, and stayed there.

His father and mother stood on the depot platform at Indian Gap, ready to welcome him. You could tell in a second that Lefty was his father's son. The older man had the same broad shoulders and long arms, identical clear hazel eyes and straw-colored hair. However, Tarbin senior did not have much hair left.

"Hello, Lefty boy!" His father's voice came booming across the station platform. There was no sign of the anger that was in his voice at the time of the long-distance call to Bolton.

"Hello, Dad. Hi, Mom!" Lefty shook hands with his dad and kissed his mother. She was a slender, well-dressed woman of middle age, her hair graying slightly.

She turned a worried look to his injured leg. "Are you sure the leg is coming along all right?"

"Swell!" he said, moving along on it to reassure her. "It will be as good as new before long."

His father nodded his head vigorously and looked a little proud. "Nothing like a broken bone could ever stop a Tarbin. No, sir!"

Lefty suspected that the older man was less concerned about the broken leg—it would mend in time—than about what Lefty was doing when he broke it.

They drove home in the family sedan, talking incessantly of everything under the sun except baseball. Lefty still cautiously avoided that subject, as he knew his father was doing.

It was great to see the old sights, to hear the pound of hammers and the calls of workmen on a new business block his father's firm was putting up, and to renew old acquaintances.

"I think I'll just forget baseball and relax," Lefty told himself privately.

He knew he could not do that entirely. Home town fans would not allow it. Local sports writers already had interviewed him. And the mail almost every day delivered a copy of the Blue River *Transcript*. The Eagles had bought him a subscription to that paper. He followed the fortunes of his old teammates with keen interest and wistful regret that he was not still with them.

A few days after his arrival in Indian Gap, he was sitting in the cool of the evening on the screened porch. Traffic moved sedately by on the shaded residential street, and the smell of Idaho summer hung in the quiet of the air. All this could be his, this friendly, comfortable life, if he wished to stay home and take a job with the Tarbin Construction Company. But he shook his head at the thought. For him only the taste of infield dust in his throat, the crack of good solid ash against horsehide, and the feel of sharp spikes digging into the dirt beneath his feet—only these thrills could he live by. Baseball was deep in his blood.

His parents were talking inside the house. As usual, Mr. Tarbin was holding forth about the construction business. Then Lefty heard his mother come into the front hall, and he knew she was standing at the screen door.

"Doesn't it feel good to be home again, Bruce?" she asked.

Home, Sweet Home, in Idaho

He smiled slightly. His mother was about the only one who ever called him Bruce any more.

"Yes, Mom," he said. "But I'll be happy to be back with the Eagles again in the spring."

The jangle of the telephone broke into their talk. Mrs. Tarbin answered it, and then said, "Bruce, it's for you."

Lefty came in and took the phone. There was a deep, solid voice on the other end. Lefty recognized the tones of Henry Brown. Henry was local American Legion head, and a pal of Tarbin senior. Like an old soldier, Brown came to the point fast.

"Lefty boy, we're in a pickle. You know Andy Myles, who's been coachin' the Junior Legion team? Well, they lugged him to the hospital this mornin'. Appendicitis. Emergency operation. Yeah, sure, Andy's doing fine. But here it is mid-season, the first of August, and the boys are hung up without a coach. Can ya help us out?"

Lefty thought fast. Unconsciously he shifted his weight onto his mending left foot. There was only a slight twinge. He could move around enough to coach the kids and help them out of this spot, couldn't he? He had intended beginning some exercise with the leg soon anyway.

"We don't wanna ask you to do anything to hurt that leg of yours, Lefty. But—"

Here was a chance to do something for the home town folks. They were behind him one hundred per cent in his own baseball bid. And he would be back in the game again, in a manner of speaking.

"Wadda ya say, Lefty?"

His answer came swiftly. "Okay, Henry," he said. "Count me in. When do I take over?"

The man on the other end chuckled delightedly. "Tomorrow afternoon. You're playin' Milford on our field then."

Things always seemed to start the hard way for Lefty. Here he was launching a spell as coach without even having a chance to see his team work out first!

He met the players at ten o'clock next morning in the high school locker room. Most of them he already knew slightly. He told them quietly that he would do the best he could to help them finish the season successfully. For that afternoon's game, however, he would let Sam Watson, catcher and captain, run the team.

Sam, a bulky, hard-driving backstop, stepped right in and ran things with surprising poise and confidence. As play began, Lefty eyed each player appraisingly. Most of the boys, he saw immediately, weren't far beyond the junior high school stage. They played improvised baseball. None of them thought very far ahead, and even Sam, a smarter player than most of the rest, failed to get the fielders in position for the pitches he called. On one occasion Sam called for an outside curve to a right-handed batter, and the second baseman played too far to his right. Lefty motioned him the other way, but the youngster still did not move far enough toward first. The ball went between first and second for a safe hit.

Plenty of other mistakes showed up during the game. Yet Lefty scolded nobody. He gave each player a bit of advice with the hope that it would sink in. As the game went on, his thoughts flashed back to the coaches and managers who had labored to make a ball player out of him. He began to understand a little bit of how Cy Benteen felt. His face reddened when he thought of the time he had disobeyed the runty manager's order to bunt.

"It's a wonder Benteen didn't skull me," he thought. "What a bush trick I played!"

Indian Gap lost the ball game, but Lefty felt no discouragement about it. There were some promising players in the group. Andy Myles had obviously worked hard with them; here and there the good effects showed up. But their performance was of the in-and-out variety. They needed lots of practice and patient coaching. He frankly told them that, and was pleased with their reaction.

Sam Watson spoke for the team.

"You show us what to do, Coach, an' we'll bust our necks tryin' to do it," the husky catcher promised.

The boys did just that. By the next week's game, they had absorbed a lot of baseball knowledge, and did not make some of their former grammar school mental errors. True, they lost the game again.

Yet their timing at bat was better, and they played enemy hitters more wisely. This team would not get into the State Legion tournament—it was too late to improve their record that much—but they would play improved baseball from here on.

Lefty's leg kept feeling better all the time. By mid-August he was jogging easily around the high school cinder track. At month's end, he was shagging flies in the outfield and taking batting practice with the Legion team.

Apparently he possessed some coaching skill, because the Indian Gap team steadily improved. For their season closer, they played Hamlin at home. Hamlin stood on about even terms with Forestville to receive the county bid to the State Tournament. Forestville played that same day, and either team could win or lose its tournament invitation on the result of this final game.

Sam Watson said, "Gang, I got nothin' against those Hamlin guys, nor in favor of Forestville. But I don't wanna see Hamlin go to that tournament at our expense!"

The locker room instantly filled with loud cheers of agreement.

Lefty grinned broadly. "That's the spirit, boys! No real ball team ever quits, no matter how much or how little any one game means to them. Knock off this Hamlin bunch this afternoon, an' I'll say we've had a darn successful season."

Home, Sweet Home, in Idaho

He did not feel too confident of an Indian Gap victory after the first two innings, though. Hamlin squeezed across a run in the first, and in the second a home run with one on gave the visitors a 3-0 lead.

Surprisingly, the Indian Gap defense tightened after that shaky start. In the fifth, little Ed Garns, who under Lefty's tutelage had developed an amazing camera eye at the plate, worked the pitcher to a three-and-two count and then let an outside curve go by for the fourth ball. There were no outs.

The second batter laid down a quick bunt to advance Garns to second. Lefty told Bobby Aldo to hit, and then flashed Ed the hit-and-run sign. It worked as far as Ed was concerned, because on the resulting grounder to second he easily took third. But the Hamlin second baseman was too smart to be caught out of position. He managed to reach the daisy cutter at his left, and erased Bobby at first. Ed wisely decided to hold third. Two away now.

Lefty called time and took Sam Watson, who batted cleanup, and Ed into conference. He intended to tell Sam to try to punch out a single instead of swinging for the fence. The team needed three runs to tie; therefore the normal play would be to hit away and hope for a cluster of runs. But the way the Hamlin moundsman was going, Sam might simply fly to the outfield.

Then, Sam himself spoke up.

"I think I can hit this guy, but it would still be only one run. Le's try some stragedy, Coach. The infield will be 'way back, an' I'm s'posed to be a power hitter. S'pose I bunt, and squeeze Ed in? It's still one run, an' they'll be so surprised they'll maybe get caught flat-footed, and I can get down to first base safe, too."

Lefty almost laughed in Sam's earnest, sweaty face. It was a crazy idea. No sane player would try it under the present conditions, with his own team three runs behind and two outs. No team tries to bunt with two outs. Then he hesitated. Sam had tried to show some baseball savvy. The backstop's brains were working, and he was willing to play a daring hunch. Why not let him try? Even if the scheme backfired, Sam would thereby learn a valuable lesson. Besides, the bulky catcher, in addition to hitting well, was fast for his size and a good bunter. Maybe he could get away with it. It was worth trying.

"Okay!" Lefty agreed crisply. "But remember, this bunt's gotta be good!"

Ed trotted back to third. Sam dug his spikes deep into the dirt at home plate, jiggled his rear in the odd way he had that always made the spectators laugh, and held his bat away back and long as though sighting for the distant fences.

Hamlin's pitcher took some dirt, rubbed it on the ball, and watched calmly as his fielders all moved back. No need to worry about the runner.

He'd die on third when this Watson either grounded out or flied out. Hamlin's pitcher smiled a little to himself.

Sam played his "stragedy" to the hilt. A fast ball came in, *zing*, too high, but Sam waved his black war club at it in a vicious swing, purposely missing. Hamlin's pitcher permitted himself a wide grin. This was duck soup. Why not strike this guy out?

Sam read his mind. The next pitch would be a wide curve. It was, and a ball. He let it go by.

Lefty watched Sam touch the visor of his cap, the bunt sign. Ed Garns saw it too out there on third, and crept a little nearer home.

The crucial pitch came in, letter high and close to a right-hand batter. Sam swayed back as if to wind up for a power swing. Then, as the ball came in, he slid his right hand up to the center of the bat. He barely touched the top of the smoke ball, and it bounced slowly along the third base line.

Ed had moved with the pitch. To nip him at the plate was impossible. But with two out, there was still a chance to nullify the run by getting Sam at first. Had the third baseman not been back on the grass, it could easily have been done. By the time he had charged in, fielded the bunt, and thrown, however, Sam was across the bag safely.

The home fans shrieked their approval at the surprise maneuver. Lefty himself felt warm and pleased over the play. He began to understand how managers and coaches sweated and strained with their players. The tension on the sidelines was worse than being out there on the field.

The play upset Hamlin, and in the next inning the Gappers scored another run. Yet, going into the ninth, it was still a 3-2 ball game, with Hamlin out front.

An explosion came in the first of the ninth. With one out, a Hamlin runner reached second on a double. He took a big lead off the bag, and Sam called for a pitchout. On the pitch, however, the runner promptly set sail for third. Sam just as promptly fired the ball to Les Blaine at third, and the Hamlin base thief was called out.

It was a close play, but no trouble appeared likely. Then suddenly the runner leaped to his feet and threw several punches at Blaine. He apparently thought Blaine had kicked him as he lay on the ground.

Lefty had been watching the action closely. Blaine stumbled as he made the tag, and in recovering his balance had accidentally brought his foot against the Hamlin man's leg. The volatile Hamlinite was banished from the game. Blaine, who wisely kept his head, received no punishment.

The rumpus subsided, and play resumed. Hamlin failed to score again, and Indian Gap went into its last time at bat trailing by a single run.

The banished Hamlin athlete was their center fielder. Now a substitute was out there in his place. The substitute hauled down a long fly ball from the

Home, Sweet Home, in Idaho

first Gap hitter, but it was easy to see that he was far from the ball hawk that the other player was.

Lefty told his boys, "Try for a long smash to center field. It could get away from that kid out there. Something like that may be all we need."

The next batter doubled, putting the tying run on second with one out. Would the run be pushed across the plate? The clamor of the mob subsided as Bobby Aldo struck out. Bobby came back to the bench almost in tears. Only one putout to go.

Sam Watson came to bat again. Lefty said, "Hit it a mile, Sam. Into center field."

Sam nodded in eager agreement. There was a light of keen understanding and determination in his eyes. This spot called for power, not "stragedy."

The power he possessed in abundance. He let the first pitch go past. Too high. Then he stepped into a curve that hung for a brief moment over the outside corner. The crack of wood on horsehide sounded all over the park. At second, the runner bent his head and took off for a non-stop flight home.

Lefty's heart jumped to his throat. Was the ball long gone? It seemed to hang for an eternity in the clear air, lacking enough power to get over the fence. There was a chance that Hamlin's substitute center fielder would pick it off the high board barrier, if he had the courage and the skill.

The sub possessed all the courage he needed, but not quite enough speed and skill. He nearly did it. But as he reached the boards, he crashed against them and lost the ball. Sam ran like mad. The luckless fielder was too dazed to pick up the horsehide, but the left gardener chased and grabbed it, then threw in desperation to the plate. Sam slid in safely by a yard.

Final score: Indian Gap 4, Hamlin 3.

Lefty owned the town of Indian Gap after that. The Legion threw a banquet for the team that, it seemed, nearly every local resident attended. Except Lefty's father. He still would not have anything to do with baseball.

September came, and then the months of fall winged swiftly by. From the Blue River *Transcript* Lefty learned that the Eagles won their pennant, and also the five-game post season series with Ashland of the Tri-River League. He winced as he read the accounts. Tom Silk's name was in all the box scores at first base. Except for bad luck, it might have been Lefty Tarbin!

Presently in mid-December came some really big news. Whitey Whelan, riding the crest of the baseball wave, was promoted to manager of the Beaumont Roughnecks in the Texas League. Whitey, then, still was in the Tiger organization; for the Roughnecks, Lefty knew, were a Tiger farm.

His heart sank a little at the announcement. With Whitey gone from Blue River, where would Lefty stand in the shuffle? Would a new manager demote

Home, Sweet Home, in Idaho 99

him, or perhaps even fire him? He saw himself starting the long, tough climb all over again. His morale sagged, and he took long walks about the countryside to get the worry off his mind.

Meanwhile his talks with his father had sometimes come very close to a discussion of Lefty's future. Occasionally Lefty had a mild hope that his father might be weakening in his opposition to a professional baseball career. One day, just before Christmas, Mr. Tarbin came home with a telegram.

"I was in the Western Union office sending out a rush order," he explained, "when I overheard the clerk say he was coming up here with this message for you, Lefty. So I took it. I was on my way home anyway."

The telegram was still sealed, and Lefty's fingers trembled as he opened it.

Just then his mother came into the room. "What is it?" she inquired. "Good news, I hope."

Lefty did not answer. The dateline on the telegram showed that it was from Detroit. Quickly he ran his eyes over the lines of print. Then, when the full import of the words broke upon him, he let out a yell.

"Wow—ee! It's from Whitey Whelan. He says I'm to report March 15 at Tucson, Arizona, for spring training."

His father's voice was cold and dry. "Are you still with the Eagles?"

"No, the Eagles don't train in Arizona. I've got

a promotion. I've been sent to Beaumont, in the Texas League!"

Lefty kissed the yellow paper in delirious joy. He moved about the room, testing his left ankle. It did not hurt a bit. He flung his arms about his mother and hugged her tightly.

Then he turned toward his dad. Maybe now—

But Lefty's eager face clouded with disappointment. He and his mother were now alone in the room. Evidently Mr. Tarbin still had no use for baseball in any form.

Well, Beaumont was a double-A team. Lefty was only one step from triple-A ball, and only two steps from the major leagues. This thing called life suddenly seemed mighty sweet again.

If only his dad—

CHAPTER VIII

PEPPER-POT INFIELD

ON THE train ride to Tucson the following spring, Lefty still marvelled over his good luck. He had not expected promotion to double-A so fast. A letter had arrived from Whitey, telling the winter's news and plans for a successful campaign at Beaumont.

"I'm bringing up Art Gray and Jackie Kent," Whitey wrote. "The Roughnecks didn't do so well in the Texas League last season. There will be plenty of jobs open. I'm relying on players like Art, Jackie, and you to pep up Beaumont baseball."

Presently a colored porter came down the aisle, his white teeth showing in a dazzling grin. He knew Lefty was a ball player.

"Only one houah from Tucson," the porter said. "You-all be out on that ball field right soon, suh."

Lefty said, "Thanks. Can't be too soon for me."

He got off the train as fast as he could and taxied to the hotel. Stepping into the lobby, he saw Whitey talking to the room clerk. The manager spotted him instantly and came right over.

"You look swell, Lefty! Seems like ages since I've seen you. Come up to my room an' we'll talk."

On the way up in the elevator, they briefed each other on events of the past months. "That pennant at Blue River last year made us all," Whitey said. "I haven't forgotten what you did, gettin' us off to a good start. That's why I want you at Beaumont."

As they entered the manager's room, Lefty could not hold back the big question in his mind.

"What's become of Tom Silk?"

Whitey eyed him closely, then laughed. "Worried about Silk, eh? Well, yuh needn't be. We sent him to the Oklahoma City Indians. Didn't like to do it, 'cause he's a power hitter. But I had two reasons. First, I needed Vic Sedgman, an O. C. pitcher. The Indians were willin' to get rid of him 'cause he's temperamental. But they held out for Silk in return. So, that's how we got Sedgman. He's a real good southpaw, which is what we need."

"And the second reason?"

"The second reason. Well, I'm bankin' on a guy named Lefty Tarbin for the first basing and longball hittin' we gotta have to move up in the league."

Lefty parried the compliment and said, "I'm still afraid of Tom. With the Indians, his bat will be working against us. He'll still be in the same league."

Whitey shrugged and was about to comment when someone knocked. "Come on in!"

The door opened and two well-set young fellows walked in. One was tall and broad-shouldered, with a mass of curly blonde hair. He sported a good-natured smile. The other was shorter, waddled a little as he walked, and looked sharply about him as though ready to pounce on something.

Lefty jumped up. "Art! Jackie!"

Art Gray and Jackie Kent came across the room.

"What you lookin' for, Kent?" Whitey chuckled. "A sneak bunt?"

Jackie reddened a little. Sober, serious at all times, he could not get used to being kidded. Not even after several seasons with pro ballplayers. Everyone shook hands.

Whitey got serious. "I wanna talk to you guys. Mostly you're the only ones I know personally on this Roughnecks team. Some of the others played against us in single-A ball, but I don't know 'em too well."

He paused and leaned forward.

"I'm plannin' to build a club with team spirit. It will have to be a unit, not just a collection of individuals. Anyone who wants to play for himself alone will be sent on his way. That's another reason that I brought you three along from Blue River. Silk was an individual player. A good one, but too anxious about Silk's battin' average, not the team's won-lost record. You guys are different. If you stay that way, you'll stick."

"I think we'll stick," Art said quietly.

That night they took in a show. Next morning everyone showed up at the field. It was spacious and neat enough, better than most training grounds Lefty had seen. What he liked about it especially was the generous area outside the base lines to chase foul flies.

Whitey introduced them to Lucky Lanning, his third base coach. Lefty took an instant dislike to Lanning, who looked shifty and hostile. He reminded Lefty of Cy Benteen. But Lanning was a veteran coach, and Whitey would not have chosen him if he were not competent.

There were not as many players in the squad as Lefty had expected. Whitey explained that for several seasons the Roughnecks had lost money, and the owners had decided to go along with as few rookies as possible. There were enough candidates for two full teams, though, and nearly a dozen pitchers. This was a fairly numerous crop of hurlers. Lefty hoped that out of the crew would come a few really good ones.

Vic Sedgman, one-time Oklahoma City glamour boy, was the prize of the mound corps, no doubt about that. He had some big league experience, was still young, and possessed supreme confidence. If only he could keep his temper under control (Lefty winced as he thought of that word "temper") he could be the bellwether of the Roughnecks.

Sedgman illustrated his potential worth in a

five-inning practice game at the end of the first week. Lefty and Jackie were in the Regulars infield, while Art filled in at first base for the Yannigans. Sedgman, still needing lots of time to perfect his control, was going the full five innings for the Yannigans.

"All's he needs is work," Jackie told Lefty. "I've read plenty 'bout him. He's wild as a hawk the first week or two, but he always seems to have his stuff an' speed when the season begins."

"Speed and stuff" was right. The first time Lefty batted against him, Sedgman gave a base on balls. But not until Lefty had nearly broken his back on two of the wickedest curve balls this side of the big leagues. As for speed, Sedgman's fireball travelled like something under jet propulsion.

One thing good, Lefty reflected grimly as he tossed aside his stick and jogged to first. Batting against this guy here in training will help me get ready for the pitching I'm bound to see when I move up into faster company.

Later that day he caught one of Sedgman's fast ones and drove it into the far outfield. But he swung late, and the ball barely dropped fair in deep left for a double.

Only a few more days passed before Whitey chose his probable opening lineup. Forced to play as short-handed as possible by the owners, the cagy manager doubled up wherever he could. Lefty played first base, but Art Gray got plenty of work there in case Lefty was hurt. Otherwise Art covered center field like a blanket.

Jackie Kent won the third-base job hands down. Strangely enough, serious Jackie was a constant chatter-box on the field, and he refused to allow the other infielders to be quiet. He goaded slick-fielding veteran shortstop Tad Reno into being talkative just to get Jackie off his neck. Second baseman Joe Gates jawed constantly, an immense wad of bubble gum bulging out his cheek day and night.

Lefty himself caught the spirit. Gates, a small but very aggressive Georgian, had a piercing whistle, punctuated frequently by his shrill, high-pitched Southern yell. Even Lefty found himself shrieking, "Hi-yah! Eee—*yah!* Yip, yip!" in Gates' manner at the batters.

Before the season opened, sports writers had dubbed them the "pepper-pot infield." Gates was proud as punch over the name. "We ain't gonna let anybody ferget it, either," he boasted.

Presently the Roughnecks left Tucson and were in Beaumont waiting to open the championship season at home against Shreveport. Then something happened, even before league play began, that nearly wrecked the infield, as far as Lefty was concerned.

Someone from a local charity asked him to visit the Home for Crippled Boys, up near the State capital, one evening. Lefty, thinking of the boys at home in Indian Gap, readily consented to go.

Pepper-Pot Infield

The charity chairman offered transportation both ways in his automobile.

Modest as usual, Lefty decided to keep mum about the visit. To be known as a publicity hound was what he most dreaded. So he said nothing to anyone, certain he would be back at the hotel in plenty of time to beat Whitey's very strict eleven o'clock deadline. They left Beaumont right after supper in the chairman's car.

His talk made a big hit with the youngsters. Presently the visit was over and they started home with time to waste. But half way back there was a flat tire, and it developed that the car had no spare. By the time a garageman was reached and the flat repaired, Lefty knew he could not make the deadline. It was eleven-thirty when he entered the hotel.

Later he wished that he had gone immediately to Whitey and explained. Instead, since the chairman let him off at the hotel's rear entrance, he decided to go up quietly in the back elevator and forget about it.

A grinning colored elevator man winked at him as he entered. On the ride up, he handed Lefty a brand new ball which already bore several autographs.

"Put yore Jawn Hancock on that thing, will yuh, boss?" the Negro said in wheedling tones. "I wanna take it home for my kid. See, I got me some names on it a'ready."

"Sure." Lefty saw no harm in signing. The colored man had a pen, a fact which surprised Lefty. But he signed the ball, gave it to the porter, who grinned even more widely, and got off at his floor.

In five minutes he was in bed and sound asleep.

He did not see Whitey next morning. Since he went out to do some shopping, and then rode directly to the park instead of going back to the hotel for lunch, he failed to meet the manager until he was dressing for the game. Whitey came into the locker room looking sore about something.

He said bluntly, "You signed this baseball after eleven last night. Why'd yuh break trainin' rules?"

Lefty stared, stupefied, at the ball in Whitey's hand. It was the same one he had signed for the porter the night before.

"Who—how—" he stammered.

Whitey eyed him coldly. "Lucky Lanning gave the colored boy a dollar for every autograph he got after eleven last night. It's Lucky's way of catchin' the night owls. Yeah, it was a lousy trick, but that don't change the fact you broke trainin'."

So it was Lanning's low-down trick! Lefty knew his instinctive dislike for the shifty coach had been justified. Sweat began to run down his back. This might get him thrown off the team. He could lose his big chance to move up the baseball ladder. Whitey was a nice guy, but very strict on discipline. Whitey's face was tight and cold now.

All Lefty could do was explain. He did that, and

when he was through, Whitey said, "Gimme that chairman's name."

Lefty told him. Whitey said, "I'll call him."

Lefty dressed, worried, while he waited. When Whitey came back, he said tersely, "Couldn't get him. He's outta town."

Lefty groaned. He'd at least miss the opener, the game he wanted keenly to play in. Whitey stood there, hesitant, probably hating to deliver the blow.

Suddenly Lefty had an inspiration. "Call the Boys' Home," he suggested. "They can at least tell you I was there."

It would not prove why Lefty was out late, but at least it would help explain things. Whitey hesitated, then said:

"Okay. If they say you were there, I'll take your word for the rest of it."

When Whitey came back, his face had softer lines.

"All right," he said. "They say you were up there. Prob'ly the rest is true. I'll believe it anyway." He started to walk away, then turned and continued, "Next time anything like that happens, tell me right away, will you?"

"I sure will," Lefty answered with relief. He went on the field, banging his glove. The team, looking snappy in brand new uniforms with scarlet-striped stockings, was out there ahead of him. There must have been more than seven thousand people crowded into Stuart Stadium. A capacity crowd.

There might have been twice that number, judging by the roar that went up greeting the Roughnecks.

He looked for the three other players whose names had been on the telltale horsehide. They were nowhere to be seen. Art Gray gave him the dope. Two of them, Sid Plummer and Hoot Williams, had just an hour ago been traded off to the Shreveport Sports for a left-handed pitcher. They would play for the Sports against Beaumont today. Bull Marciano, slated to be released anyway, was dropped to a club in the Sally League. Only Lefty survived the purge.

Word got around fast. *Don't fool with Whitey Whelan!*

Perhaps it was a good thing, he reflected. Every ball club needs to know just who is boss, and now there would be no more trouble of that kind on the Roughnecks. But just the same, he could not down his contempt for the method which Lucky Lanning had used. He had a hunch Lanning never would be popular with this team.

The practice ball sped unerringly around the infield as the Roughnecks completed their drill. Then the plate umpire called "Play ball!" Vic Sedgman fired his fast ball close in to the first Shreveport batter. The official yelled *"Stee—rike!"* and the new Texas League campaign was on.

For three innings no batter on either team reached first base. It began to look as though one of the hurlers might come up with a no-hitter. But not a player in either dugout breathed a word about that possibility. No one wanted to put the whammy on his own pitcher. Neither hurler was destined for the no-hitter, though. In the fourth inning, each side got a blooper hit, and the tension was off.

Lefty could feel the relief that swept over the bench. Now the athletes could concentrate on winning the game, and forget about the no-hit pressure.

Batting third, Lefty struck out his first time up. The second trip he grounded out to the first baseman. When in the sixth inning he came to the plate for the third time, it was with a greater feeling of confidence. Jerry Blanding, Shreveport twirler, depended mainly on a quick-breaking hook and a fast ball. That was plenty, but Lefty had observed already that Blanding could not fully control his change of pace.

He waited confidently for the time when Blanding would try to fool him with a change-up.

"It ought to come this trip," he thought as he dug in at the plate. "He knows I'm on to his curve and his fireball. I'm due for the change-up, sure."

The first pitch was a slow-breaking curve. Lefty let it go by, thinking it was wide. The plate official called it a strike, but Lefty did not protest. Next came a waste ball, high and wide. Then Blanding let go with his fireball. Lefty swung too late, and the ball went foul into the left-field stands.

Now he might as well get set for it. The change

of pace, that is. Blanding thought he had him off balance. Lefty remembered grimly the first time, back in college, when a foxy major leaguer in an exhibition game had made him look foolish with a tantalizing floater.

In his mind's eye he saw the Shreveport catcher holding three fingers down under his mitt, the signal for the flutter ball. Blanding stared a moment, nodded with pretended indifference, and reared back as though to launch a fast one.

The way he did it, Lefty could have sworn the ball would come in trailing smoke. But from the time it left Blanding's hand, it moved like a toy balloon. He almost went mad waiting for the white blob to reach the plate. He could almost count the stitches on the cover.

He held back, fighting an overpowering desire to unload on the serve. Then it was in there, and he swung as hard as he could.

Boom!

The ball caromed off the bat like a rocket and soared far over the outfield. It was long gone in a moment, going up and up as it passed the fence. He could see the wildly waving arms of the bleacher fans as the ball passed high over them. It disappeared in a clump of high-growing trees outside the park.

The fans nearly tore their seats up as he jogged around the bases. Everyone knew it was the longest hit ever made in Stuart Stadium—except pos-

Pepper-Pot Infield 113

sibly Babe Ruth's exhibition game home run there back in the twenties.

That single run loomed big as a house when Shreveport came to bat in the first of the ninth. Sedgman still pitched flawlessly, and the Sports had failed to get a runner beyond second.

Here Sedgman's glamour-boy complex made its first Beaumont appearance. Confident of setting down the opposition one-two-three, he pitched carelessly to the first batter. That player instantly hit the first pitch into left field for a single. The next Sport bunted him to second. It happened as fast as that.

With only one out and the tying run on second, Shreveport had a good chance to tie and even to go ahead. Sedgman, shaken a little out of his overconfidence by the turn of events, nevertheless called on his proved diamond savvy and pitched with extreme care to Earl Connors, Sport right fielder with a reputation for hitting well in the clutch.

Sedgman's infield backed him to the hilt. Looking across the diamond, Lefty saw Jackie leaning forward, pounding his fist in his glove, yelling at Sedgman to get the batter out of there. At second, Joe Gates emitted even more piercing whistles and kept up a succession of "Hip-hip-*heeyah*'s."

Tad Reno lifted a pebble from the dirt, smoothed out the spot with his foot, then darted behind the base runner to keep him near the bag. Sedgman watched out of the corner of his eye, his hands across his chest, but made no motion to pick off the runner.

Tad yelled, "Get the sucker outta there, Vic!"

Joe Gates punctuated the yell with a blood-chilling, eerie whistle.

Lefty stooped over, tense, his hands on his knees. He remembered Sam Watson's pinch bunt in the Junior Legion game, and feared that Connors, a smart cookie, might try the same thing. Yet he dared not move in too close. Connors might dunk one over his head. Brother, would that be bad!

Connors swung on the pitch. He tried to punch the ball over second, but did not get under it enough. The ground ball skidded past Sedgman's desperate lunge and headed for right center.

Gates, sprinting like a track man, went after the chopper. At the last second he stuck out his mitt, and as the ball seemed about to spurt by into the outfield, he got leather in front of it.

He put on the brakes, whirled, and fired in one motion. His throw zinged into Lefty's glove just before Connor's foot reached first base.

Meanwhile instinct told Lefty to keep his eye on the Sport going into third. He did not need the frenzied yells of seven thousand maniacs in the stands to tell him what was happening. The Sport had rounded third and was pounding for home.

Connors guessed what was happening. As he passed first base, knowing he was out, he gave Lefty the hip. The shove sent Lefty to his knees. In one

The umpire's right arm jerked up.

agonizing second he saw the runner flying toward the plate. Then, with a terrific effort, he scrambled to his feet and pegged home almost in one motion. The white flash of horsehide raced the figure in the pin-striped suit for home plate.

Ten feet away from the plate, the surging Sport left his feet. He slid into catcher Maxie Schwartz like a cannon ball smacking a dreadnaught. Maxie did not budge. He took Lefty's low throw and slammed it into the runner's gleaming spikes. The umpire's right arm jerked up.

Out!

Thanks to Beaumont's pepper-pot infield, the Roughnecks had put the opening game in the bag.

CHAPTER IX

SOS TO BOBBY DALE

THE Roughnecks were all in one bus, going to Houston. Texas Leaguers generally travel by Pullman, but on short jumps a bus sometimes is used. They had played two series at home, and now were heading out on a long road trip. Two out of four from Shreveport. That was okay. The Sports were tough cookies in any park. Then three of four from Tulsa.

Not bad. Not bad at all. Five out of eight for a .625 percentage, third in the league standings. The Sports had six of eight, beating Dallas four times. Tulsa led the league with six of seven, and had one game rained out.

"Did I ever tell you 'bout the time I got thrown out of a game for sayin' nothing?" silent Jackie Kent suddenly asked nobody in particular.

Casey Boles yelled Jackie's question over again so that everyone in the bus could hear.

"You're always sayin' nothing," Ralph Cavello chortled. "You must get thumbed out nearly every day!"

Jackie reddened. "This time I really did. It was

at Nashville. The boys were gettin' on the umpire for bum calls. He warned us to shut up. So Beans Campbell, who'd been doin' most of the yelling anyway, reaches over, plasters some white tape on my mouth, and shoves me outta the dugout. Umps takes one look, reddens up like a beet, an' out I go. First and only time it ever happened to me. That I got the heave-ho, I mean."

Everyone in the bus snickered.

Tad Reno said, "Reminds me of the time Lou Stark managed at Baltimore. Or Scranton, I forget which. I was with him both places. One day it starts to sprinkle. We're two runs ahead, but the officials won't call the game." Tad chuckled at the recollection. "So Lou gets an umbrella, opens it, an' walks out to home plate to beef. He got the thumb, but fast."

When the laughter subsided, Whitey spoke. "I don't mind a few shenanigans to help make life interestin', boys. But don't get yourselves put outta any ball games. We're in third place now, an' we can go higher."

The players grew quiet and listened.

"Tulsa's in first place now. But when things level off, they'll drop to the second division. You'll see. This is gonna be a three-team scramble. The Sports will be up there all the time—all the time, they will. But O. C. is our big headache. Them Indians have got pitchin', fieldin', and hittin'. They're the team to beat."

Casey said slyly, "Who else figgers it a three-team race, Whitey?"

Whitey looked as if he would explode.

"Look here, you guys," he snapped. "Maybe the experts don't give us a chance. I know they're callin' this a two-team show. The Indians an' Shreveport. But I also know what we got here. I know all you guys, that's what. S'pose the dopesters do figger us for sixth place, after finishin' seventh last year? Heck, this is different. Tad an' Case are the only reg'lars left from that team, except pitchers. I know what you guys can do. Let 'em call us 'fizz kids' if they wanna. We'll show 'em a thing or two; and if we ain't up there by September, I'll eat Maxie's catcher's mitt!"

The bus went silent. That kind of talk made a team feel good, Lefty thought. The confidence of a manager who will go all the way with his men can make a squad play the best ball of which it is capable—and sometimes better ball. Yes, sir, Whitey was that kind of manager, and Lefty knew that every Roughneck on the team was making a silent vow to go all out for him.

That is the way Lefty and the rest felt when they opened the long road trip at Houston. They took only two out of four games from the Buffaloes, but won three of four in the next series at San Antonio with the Missions. They were still holding onto that third spot in the league standings.

That is the kind of ball which with just a little

improvement can win pennants. But, said the sports writers, the Roughnecks are playing over their heads. 'Way over their heads. Just wait. It won't last, and the thump will be all the louder when they finally hit the second division.

The series against the Indians would tell the story. Oklahoma City was beginning to roll after a weak start. And much of the reason was Tom Silk. Lefty grimaced as he read the league batting statistics and saw Tom's steady climb. Silk's average wasn't too high, not yet above .300, but the burly Indian first sacker was hitting that long ball. He would soon be leading the league in the important runs-batted-in department. And O. C. would be leading the league, period.

Beaumont's fears of Oklahoma were justified, after the Roughnecks went there following an even split in four games at Fort Worth. Maybe it was simply awe at sight of an Indian uniform. Perhaps it was only the jitters in a young team which finds itself hanging onto a too dizzy, precarious perch. At any rate, Beaumont lost the first two games, 6-3 and 4-0. They came back to win the third, 5-4, and then dropped the series finale, 3-1.

The league standings now read: Shreveport first, Oklahoma City second, Tulsa third, and Beaumont fourth. The skidding Roughnecks were only two percentage points out of the Texas League second division. This, said the writing experts, is only what you could expect.

SOS to Bobby Dale

Whitey summoned Lefty to his hotel room before they checked out. In one hour the train would be taking them to Dallas for a series with the Eagles.

Whitey appeared grim but not downcast.

"We ain't as bad as we looked in those games, Lefty. The boys didn't hit. They choked up in the field. I wonder what's wrong!"

Lefty hesitated, and then kept silent.

Whitey paced the room. His troubled gray eyes sought the carpet. "I know, I know," he muttered. "We can all see it. The Roughnecks won't win any pennant with Tad Reno at shortstop. Is that it?"

Lefty shifted his feet and still said nothing. He did not want to stick a knife in the back of a teammate. Tad was a good guy.

"Heck, Lefty, I've known it ever since spring practice." He ignored his first baseman's sharp glance. "I've known that Tad has slowed down to a walk. He can't pick up that ball and get it to second fast enough for the DP. He can't peg to first from deep short the way he usta. In fact, on a hard-hit ball to his right, he can't even *get* to deep short!"

Lefty spoke slowly. "Does Tad know this?"

"Yeah." Whitey ran his fingers through his light hair. "He admits he's slowed down a lot, told me to take him out any time I want. But heck, Lefty, you know we haven't got another shortstop. I've combed the bushes ever since I took this job, and there ain't a shortstop I can buy or steal. Not one who'd be an improvement over Tad, anyway."

Lefty said quietly, "Maybe I can get you one."

"*What!*"

Lefty nodded. "He played with me in college. Played second base at the time, but he's really a natural shortstop. Went to second because Ed Sinsibaugh couldn't play any place else but short."

"Where's this guy now?"

"Working on his father's farm in Maine. But I've had letters from him, an' I think he'd like to take a shot at pro ball. In the past two years his father's health has improved, and a coupla younger brothers have grown up enough to take over most of the farm work. I'm sure he'd come down for a tryout."

"What's his name?"

"Dale. Bobby Dale. If I sent him a telegram, I bet we'd have him here by the time we get back to Stuart Stadium."

Whitey smiled, still a trifle grimly, as he started piling things into his suitcase.

"Send that wire right away. Tell your Bobby Dale to go direct to Beaumont, get a uniform, an' work out till we come home. That'll be about ten days. I crave a look at this 'natural' shortstop of yours!"

Lefty sent the telegram before the train departed for Dallas. He instructed Bobby to send his reply there within the next four days; or, if he could not make up his mind by that time, to Shreveport, next stop on the Roughnecks' itinerary before arriving home.

SOS to Bobby Dale

Beaumont won the first game at Dallas, and lost the second because in the last of the ninth Tad Reno was not quite fast enough getting off a double play ball.

Lefty almost forgot about that defeat when, back at the hotel, he found a telegram waiting for him. It was from Bobby and it read: "Plane leaves Boston Thursday noon. Will be ready play ball Saturday. Bobby."

Today was Wednesday. In just one week, next Wednesday, the Roughnecks opened a long home stand at Stuart Stadium against every other team in the league. With several days to work out at the stadium, Bobby should be ready to step into the lineup in the first game with Houston.

That is, if Whitey gave him an okay, and if Tad's play in the meantime did not improve enough to justify keeping the old infield together. Whitey was not overly superstitious. But when his outfit was clicking, he would hate to make a change.

Whitey was elated over Bobby's reply. He phoned the Beaumont groundskeeper to furnish Bobby with everything he needed. There always was someone around the park available to pitch to practice batters, hit grounders and fungoes and shag flies. Bobby would have all the practice he wanted.

They split the four-game Dallas series, but lost three out of four at Shreveport. Heading back home, they read newspaper stories crying that the

Roughnecks were on the skids. Sure enough, they had dropped into the second division, the Houston Buffaloes edging them out of fourth place. Only the poor play of the lower teams (Fort Worth, San Antonio, and Dallas) kept the Roughnecks as high as they were. Or so said the sports writers.

Were they really a second division club? Young and inexperienced as most of them were in double-A ball, was it too much to hope for a top spot in the league standings? These questions Lefty and the others kept asking themselves on the ride back home.

"No, it ain't too much," Tad declared emphatically in answer to the last question. "We just ain't found ourselves. All's we need is a spark. Somethin' to make us click. What that spark is, or where we'll get it, I dunno. But when it comes—watch out for the Roughnecks!"

They all nodded agreement, adding to Tad's statement with comments of their own.

Lefty thought, "If our infield can work as a unit, that will be what we need. Tad can't give it to us on the field. Maybe Bobby can."

They reached Beaumont late Monday night. The hotel desk clerk handed Whitey a written message. Whitey read it and showed it to Lefty.

"The clerk put me in 209. Come on up." It was signed by Bobby Dale.

Lefty beat his manager to the door of 209 and flung it open without knocking. A familiar, stocky figure, black-haired, lay on the bed. The figure's eyes were closed, but Lefty did not wait to discover whether the man on the bed was asleep or awake. He let out a wild Comanche yell.

Bobby came off the bed fast. He fixed his momentarily startled dark eyes on Lefty. Then his face lighted up in recognition.

Lefty grabbed his hand, slapped him on the back, and cried, "Greetings, you old stumblebum! How'd we ever get you off the farm?"

"Aw, they can spare me now," Bobby grinned. "At least for a few months—if you keep me that long!" He saw Whitey in the doorway. The manager came forward and stuck out his hand.

"I'm Whitey Whelan."

"Hello, Mr. Whelan. Glad to meet you."

Whitey and Lefty took chairs. Bobby sat on the big double bed.

Lefty said, "Have you worked out yet?"

It developed that Bobby had several workouts at the stadium. More, he told them that for a month he had been playing semi-pro ball in Maine.

"I played shortstop at home. If you want to try me there, or anywhere else, it's okay by me."

"Good!" Whitey said. "We got an off day tomorrow. There'll be a two-hour workout in the afternoon, startin' at two. See you then."

Next day at the park Whitey had a long batting and fielding drill. Then he called for a short practice game, Yannigans against the regulars.

"See if we can get back some of our timing," he grunted to Lucky Lanning. "We sure lost it somewhere on that road trip."

Tad Reno played first-team shortstop for two innings. After that, Bobby filled the spot. Lefty ambled out to first base for the third inning with a feeling of keen expectancy. He had recommended Bobby, and hoped for old times' sake as well as for the present emergency that his pal would make the grade. Yet he knew that more than a score of pairs of eyes would be fixed critically on the former Bolton College flash. Bobby was more than just another infielder to the Beaumont regulars. If he was any good, he might bring baseball glory—and pennant money—to them all.

Bobby had fielded at infield drill and looked all right. What would he do when the pressure was on? Well, the Roughnecks would get a sample of his fielding in this practice session. Lefty crossed his fingers and mumbled good luck wishes for his old college teammate.

The new regular infield snapped the ball around with lots of zip. Jackie Kent started a practice double play that went to Joe Gates on second and over to Lefty. Lefty set in motion a first-to-second-to-first DP that was a model of speed and precision. Bobby held up his end on a grounder to short to start another practice double killing.

Then the first Yannigan in the third inning came to bat. Vern Winthrop fed him a couple of fast balls, then a curve. The Yannigan dumped the curve into short right for a single.

"Get two!" Joe Gates yelled. *"Hee*-yah! Get two!"

"Pour it in, Vern boy! Let'm hit."

"In the groove, kid, in the groove! Nothin' to worry about."

Lefty shifted toward second. The Yannigan batter was right-handed, and a notorious pull hitter. Gates walked over and said something to Bobby. Bobby shifted back and to his right.

The Yannigan took a healthy swing at the first pitch. Maybe he wanted to win a regular job. Perhaps his anxiety to test Bobby's fielding ability made him place the ball just where he did. Anyway, he could not have spot-hit the pellet any more neatly to test the new shortfielder.

The hit, a sizzling grasscutter, roared past Jackie Kent's desperately outflung glove. It headed like a rocket for the open spaces of left field. And it appeared certain to go through.

Suddenly, appearing from nowhere to the astonished eyes of onlookers, a stocky figure in scarlet-striped stockings dashed for the certain base hit. Crossing the gloved hand along his body and near the ground, the figure made a desperate lunge for the ball. Still it looked as though it could not be stopped. Incredibly, though, the glove got down there and at the last split second the ball smacked in. Bobby put on the brakes, whirled, and apparently without looking shot the ball waist-high to second base.

Joe Gates speared the perfect throw, then pivoted and snap-threw to Lefty. Both runners were out by inches. You could almost hear the gasps that went up from the onlookers, Yannigans and regulars alike. The double killing was a honey. A real honey.

The next batter struck out.

Lefty said it to himself as he walked off the field, and he knew that every Roughneck from Whitey Whelan down to the bat boy was saying it, too. We've got a chance now. This is gonna be a real infield. With a DP combination like that, we've really got a chance!

Lefty saw the wide smile on Whitey's face. There was something almost pleasant, even, in Lucky Lanning's crooked grin. Tad Reno looked immensely pleased and rueful at the same time.

"Tad knows his job is gone," Lefty thought. "But he's a real team man. He's glad of it, if the team gets a better shortstop than he is. That's the Roughneck spirit."

Somebody on the bench mumbled something that sounded like "Million-dollar infield!"

CHAPTER X

OH, YOU ROUGHNECKS!

When the Texas League season is completed, there is a play-off among the teams finishing in the first four positions. The club finishing first plays the one in fourth position, and those in the second and third places have a play-off too. Then the winners of these two series meet each other. All these series are decided by the best four out of seven games.

Finally, the winner in this elimination marathon then takes on the Southern Association champion in the Dixie Series. The victorious team here must win four of seven games.

"After that," said Bobby Dale when Casey had patiently explained the system to him, "can I go home to Maine for my Christmas dinner?"

Players in the train's drawing room chuckled. The long home stand was over, and the team was en route to Dallas, after away-from-home series with Houston and San Antonio.

With the coming of Bobby the Roughnecks had caught fire. He apparently was the spark which Tad had said they needed. Lefty felt his own confidence grow. He was looser and more at home with his old Bolton teammate on the club, and his batting average climbed to .320. But the Sports, Indians, and Tulsa Oilers performed like major leaguers, too, and Beaumont still was in fourth place. Nevertheless, it was a stronger fourth, and the Oilers led them only by a game and a half. Before this road trip was over, the Roughnecks should be yammering on the tails of the second-place Indians.

At any rate, how could they fail to be in the play-offs, among the first four finishers?

"It ain't just the idea of bein' in the play-offs," Tad remarked. "Y'know, we get more money the higher we finish. So le's go for that first-place spot!"

It was a matter of pride, too. You couldn't tell anyone in the Roughneck dugout that they weren't the best club in the league. Anyway, they played like it in the Dallas opener, winning handily, 8 to 3. But the Oilers beat Houston that day, and it was still a game and a half away for Lefty and his mates.

Next day in a ten-inning hair raiser, Dallas eked out a 4-3 win. The Oilers obliged by letting the Buffaloes beat them.

In the third Beaumont-Eagles set-to, the lid blew

Oh, You Roughnecks!

off. The Roughnecks scored in clusters, winning a 12-4 game while Tulsa lost. Only a half game behind now. Then Beaumont copped the Dallas finale, Tulsa got beaten, and the Roughnecks were in third place!

Gradually the players began to develop a rollicking, confident spirit.

Even Casey caught the victory germ. He remarked one day on the ride to Fort Worth, "This-here league ain't gonna be able to stop us. Know that, Whitey? Ain't nobody in the Texas League gonna keep us from that pennant!"

Whitey's face went grim.

"Better wait till the race is over," he cautioned. "Anythin' can happen yet."

At Fort Worth, they took the first three games from the Cats and led in the fourth game, 6 to 4, going into the last of the eighth inning. Then something happened.

Lefty couldn't figure out afterwards how it all began. But after one man was out, Vic Sedgman passed the Cat shortstop. Fort Worth's manager, Hap Young, promptly lugged out a right-handed pinch batter to face the lefty Sedgman. His strategy began to pay off. The hit-and-run was on, and the batter singled behind the runner into right. The hit left men on first and third with one out.

Another right-handed pinch hitter came to the plate. Hap Young certainly was pulling out all the stops. Lefty saw Whitey fidgeting in the dugout, pulling at the bottom of his jacket in the way he always did when the going got rough. The man on first stole second. Catcher Maxie Schwartz bluffed a throw, but didn't dare let the ball go for fear the runner on third would come in. Sedgman finally gave the batter a walk.

Bases full, one out!

Whitey came out on the field. He fingered the bottom of his jacket steadily.

That was all for Sedgman. The glamour boy protested, threw his glove on the turf. Ten thousand Fort Worth fans yowled and screamed insults. Whitey was adamant. Sedgman went out, and right-handed Ace Marshall came in.

Lefty, watching the proceedings from his position astride first base, wondered how the switch would work. Probably Ace would see only rightie hitters, because Young had loaded his lineup with them to get Sedgman out of there. With the top of the batting order coming up, he probably would not insert any more pinch hitters.

That was the way things developed; but it was bad medicine for the Roughnecks just the same. The next Cat fanned. Then Bones McLowery, the best place hitter on the Cats, with power to boot, clouted a screaming liner into left center between Casey and Art Gray. When Art got the ball back to the infield, three runs were over, McLowery stood triumphantly on third, and the Cats led, 7 to 6.

Oh, You Roughnecks!

"It's the showers for Marshall," Lefty thought.

So it was. Another right-handed reliefer, Fritz Obler, trudged across the grass from the bull-pen, his warm-up jacket slung carelessly over his right shoulder. The bat boy ran out for the jacket. Fritz took his three warm-up pitches, Whitey standing there watching. Lefty strolled over to listen. The next batter, very tall and rangy, swung three heavy bats near the plate.

"This guy, this Koslowskas," Whitey was saying, "murders a fast ball, high. Keep him low an' close, break off a curve, then give him the change-up." He started to walk off the mound, turned and came back. "Remember. Pitch him low an' close first!"

The infielders surrounded Obler.

"Koslowskas is a rightie," Jackie said. "If he hits the close ball, Bobby gets it, or me. The curve, it goes to Lefty or Joe. The change-up—"

Obler rubbed the ball on his uniform and grinned. He seemed unperturbed.

"—the change-up," he finished, "if he hits it, you infielders don't worry. It goes over the fence!"

Obler teased the batter with an outside ball. Then Koslowskas missed one low and close. Strike one. He let an almost identical pitch go by, and the umpire called it a strike. Koslowskas screamed to the sky, but the count stood one ball, two strikes.

Lefty moved back a little and closer to the line. According to plan, Obler's next offering would be an outside curve. If this big moose connected late, it could be a rough hot shot down the right-field foul line. Cautiously the entire infield shifted with Lefty. Hap Young saw the maneuver and sensed what kind of pitch was coming in. He yelled to Koslowskas.

The rangy guy heard the yell. He started to swing, tried to stop, then chose to follow through. The crack of bat against ball sounded all over the park. It was a late swing and Koslowskas practically stole the ball out of the catcher's mitt. The white blur went like a jet toward Lefty.

Lefty brought his crab-net over and stabbed for the flying ball. He lost his balance, fell on his face, and never even saw the pellet go by him. He scrambled up, expecting to see Koslowskas bearing down on him.

Then he sighed with relief. The umpire was chopping with his right arm toward the stands along first. Foul ball!

That was a break for the Roughnecks, because Koslowskas turned out to be a prize sucker for the change-up after all. He swung, missed, fell on his backside, and the Cats were retired.

"Seven to six. We gotta get that run," they puffed as they trooped into the dugout. "Gotta get two to win. Let's go!"

"Let's go, hey!"

Whitey called out, "Gray—Tarbin—Boles!

Oh, You Roughnecks!

C'mon, shake it up, you guys. One run to tie. Two to win. C'mon, we can do it!"

That was the kind of manager to play ball for. He had confidence in you, and you couldn't help giving that extra jigger of moxie.

Art Gray struck out.

It's up to me, Lefty thought. Heck, it's up to me. Get on base, that's all. One of the gang will bring me in.

He'd been having a hard time with Ozzie Colman out there on the mound, though. Bad enough that Ozzie was a right-hander. Worse, he had a mean curve that broke in sharp on Lefty. Two strike-outs, and a grounder to short. That's all Lefty had for the day so far.

The first one was too wide. Then that terrific incoming hook. Lefty swung late and fouled it off. One and one. What would Ozzie burn in next? A change of pace? That would be normal to expect. No, Ozzie was too cute. He'd figure Lefty would watch for the floater. Heck, he'll try to cross me up with another hook, I bet. Well—

It came burning in, looking like a letter-high smoke ball. Then, just as it reached the plate, it broke down and in to a left-handed batter.

Lefty anticipated the sharp break of the ball. He stepped forward and swung just as the hook started to snap off.

Crack!

He had come around with his bat a little early. He regularly pulled a ball to right, anyway. This time Colman's pitch came in so fast that, even though he undercut the ball slightly, it sizzled into right field without much height.

Lefty dug in for first. The whole scene was directly before him as he ran. The first baseman dancing back to the bag. Cat right fielder running in mad desperation for the sinking liner. Wild, hoarse yells from the stands. The dry air rushing in gasps into his lungs. Agonizing dread that the fleet fielder would spear the line drive.

The liner sank abruptly to the grass, a foot inside the line, as though pulled down by a powerful, invisible magnet. It ticked the right fielder's glove as it fell, then rolled over the line and against the stands in foul territory. Lefty, rounding first, saw it take a crazy bounce off the barrier.

Now he could no longer see the play. He dug in for second, cleats biting the dirt, head down, flying like a scared prairie dog before wolves.

Dig in, kid, dig in. This is the tying run!

He lifted his head long enough to see the second sacker raise his arms as if anticipating the oncoming throw. Was he faking? There was no time to guess. Ten feet away, Lefty dived head first for the bag. Dry, choking dust spurted into his mouth, nose, and eyes as though from a hundred geysers of dirt. The thud when he hit the ground knocked out his breath. He slid along on his belly, feeling like

Oh, You Roughnecks!

a hornpout being dragged across a pebbly shore. His groping fingers clutched for the bag, found only hard earth, clutched wildly further, and then in the end struck canvas.

Whether he was safe or not, he did not know. He was enveloped in a typhoon of swirling, gritty dirt that he could taste. He could scarcely breathe. But he clung for dear life to that square of sawdust-packed canvas.

Finally the dust commenced to settle. He dragged himself onto the base, sat down, began brushing himself off. As things cleared he saw the Cat second baseman and shortstop, their chests shoved up against the umpire, chins wagging furiously. The first baseman came running up, waving his arms. Hap Young scrambled from the dugout. An angry, ominous roar grew in the stands.

Looks like I'm safe, all right!

The rhubarb lasted nearly five minutes. The base umpire wouldn't change his decision. Twice he stalked off. Twice he motioned again, emphatically, with his palms flattened toward the ground. Boo upon resentful boo rolled down from the packed stands. Then Hap Young reluctantly got off the field, stopping several times to yap back at the object of his wrath. The infielders took their stations, and play began once more.

One out. A single will bring me in, and here's ol' Case to do it.

Casey let the first pitch go by. Ball one. Then

Colman tried a letter-high fast ball. Casey watched it come smoking down the pike. It was in close, but Casey's tight stance allowed him to shift quickly on any pitch. He stepped back with his left foot, brought his bat around with all the power in his wide shoulders, and creamed the fireball.

It rose in a high arc for the center field bleachers. Lefty, dancing far off second, felt sure it was in there for a homer. Then he wasn't sure. He scuttled back and tagged up. If the ball went in, he would of course score. If not, he must be prepared to advance on the catch. He played it safe.

Would the darn skyscraper never come down? At last it stopped rising and began to descend. A chorus of "oh's" and "ah's" arose from the fans.

The center fielder stood with his back against the low wall. Suddenly, as the ball appeared about to drop in for a four-master, the fielder stuck up his glove. The blob of white smacked leather and settled comfortably into the pocket. Casey had been robbed of a home run by a real world series catch.

Meanwhile, as the ball hit leather, Lefty was off. He bore down on third with all the speed he could muster. He knew he had the throw beaten easily. But a daring thought was in his mind. The center fielder, held for an instant against the rail in the need for holding onto the ball, could not regain his balance in time for a fast throw. In fact, he could never make the peg all the way home without

Oh, You Roughnecks!

a relay. And that relay, Lefty grimly determined, he could beat to the plate.

Lucky Lanning, coaching at third, apparently had the same idea. Or he quickly picked it up when he saw Lefty fail to apply the brakes. Anyway, Lanning promptly flashed the green light.

Lefty rounded third at full speed. His way was clear to the plate, and he dug in hard. Half-way home, though, his legs began to get heavy. He caught a glimpse of several figures in travelling gray Roughneck uniforms behind the plate, frantically waving him in. Beaumont players were spilling out of the dugout. One of the Roughnecks behind the plate kept pounding with his fist, index finger pointing down, toward the dirt.

Slide, kid, slide! Hit the dirt!

The oversized Cat backstop smacked his fist in his glove. He had the plate blocked, his mask off, and his gaze rivetted on deep short. Lefty saw his face light up expectantly. The relay was on the way in.

He took off in a reckless, spikes-high slide. He hit the catcher with every ounce of weight and power in his six-two frame. They went down in a wild tangle, the ball squirted out of the Cat's big mitt, and the umpire—his hand already on its way up for the out sign—changed his mind, levelled his palms, and yelled, "Safe!"

The irate crowd erupted with malignant yells

and screams. Then gradually the sound died away, as it does when a home team play has failed to halt the enemy, and was succeeded by a sullen, angry silence.

The Roughnecks nearly pounded the life out of Lefty in their mad glee. Then Jackie Kent grounded into the third out, and the Cats came in for the last of the ninth.

They could not score. The game dragged into the tenth, eleventh, and twelfth innings. Then, in the thirteenth, the Roughnecks tallied on a pass, a bunt, and a single by Ralph Cavello. The Cats could not match that marker, and Beaumont had the game, 8 to 7, for a clean sweep of the series.

Everyone talked about Lefty's feat that evening.

Whitey said, "I saw Pepper Martin pull the same thing when we were together on the Gas House Gang, back in thirty-six; or thirty-seven, maybe it was. I don't know which. It was up at Braves Field, I remember."

Ol' Hoss Roper, the pitching coach, sucked on his briar pipe and said, "I seen it done more'n once, in the old days. Fact is, it was done agin me. But Ol' Hoss never seen it done better'n Lefty pulled it off today. No, sirree."

Finally Casey, who had been sitting in moody silence, spoke up.

"It sure was the best piece of base runnin' I ever did see." He paused a moment, then inquired plaintively, "But heck, if I'da caught that-there pitch solid, there'd been no need for Lefty to slide. I'da had me a easy home run. What'm I gonna do about that, Tad? I ain't been meetin' the ball square lately. Got any suggestions?"

Tad spoke carefully. "Yeah, maybe I got an idea, Case."

The veteran outfielder edged forward eagerly. "What is it?"

Tad hesitated for the briefest second and then advised solemnly:

"Don't worry about meetin' the pitch solid. When the ump ain't lookin', just put a pair of wings on the ball, so it'll carry over the fence!"

CHAPTER XI

FIFTEEN THOUSAND
RABBITS' FEET

BLISTERING hot weather, bugbear of many a diamond athlete, came on fast. Stifling, power-draining heat that left the players feeling like moist dishrags after every game. But the Roughnecks were young and had sinews like rubber bands. They bounded back each day with as much pep as they had the day before.

And they climbed in the standings. By mid-July they were in a knock-down, drag-out fight for second place with Oklahoma City. In August they passed the Indians and challenged Shreveport for the top.

"It's a blame good thing we got that kid Dale," Tad said. "My dogs never woulda taken the gaff every day. This is the hottest summer I ever did see."

Lefty continued to play good ball. True, he once let the old Tarbin temper get the better of him, and took part in a brawl at first base with Andy Sevino of the Missions. But each player got off with a small fine and a three-day suspension.

He often thought of his father. His hopes were still strong that if he made his way into the big time and stayed, Tarbin senior would forget his mysterious hatred of the game.

Lefty himself knew that he was the happiest he could ever be. This was the life for him. He had done right in refusing to take a job in his father's construction business. Some day, he assured himself, Dad will get over being sore for what I've done and will realize what a great thing baseball is.

He admitted that his father must be very narrow-minded. Could not the older man guess how much Lefty had been hurt at his dad's anger when the son had made a decision of his own?

These thoughts did not interfere with his work on the diamond. He fought like a tiger with the rest of the gang to pass Shreveport. Yet fate—in the form of Lefty's old nemesis, Tom Silk—deprived the Roughnecks of that satisfaction. On the last day of the season, Silk beat the Roughnecks in Stuart Stadium with a ninth-inning home run. The Sports won their game at Houston, and finished in first place by a half-game over Beaumont.

"Never mind that," Whitey told them. "We're in the play-offs, an' we can win 'em if we play heads-up ball. That's all we need. Heads-up ball, and keep fightin' every minute."

Because of their second place finish, they met the third-place Indians first. Despite Tom Silk's big bat, Beaumont won four of the first six games and the right to meet Shreveport in the final series. The Sports had no trouble eliminating Tulsa's Oilers.

That final Texas League play-off marathon was, in the words of a sports writer, "a ring-tailed lulu." It dragged out to seven games, with none of the first six being decided by more than two runs.

Going into the last inning of the seventh game, played at Beaumont, the Roughnecks trailed by one run. With Lefty on first after a pass, Casey singled through the hole on the hit-and-run. Lefty, instead of stopping at second, took Lanning's signal from third to keep coming.

As he rounded second, the Sports shortstop gave him the hip. Lefty stumbled, lost his stride, but did not fall. He was sore enough to halt and slug the offender. Instead, he dug in and tried to make third.

Probably it was the boiling anger inside him that made him do it. Too, the Roughnecks had to have this run. Anyway, he came in with a high slide, spikes flashing in the sun, and made a hard stab for the bag as he landed.

The ball and the runner came into third together. The fielder slapped his glove on Lefty, but the slide was so bone-crushing that fielder and ball spilled over into the coach's box. The white horsehide fell out of the glove and lay on the ground. That's where the third baseman ended up, too.

Harry Bell, hurling for Shreveport, backed up the play, and Lefty had no chance to break for home. Casey went into second easily. Bell had no chance to cut him down. So what he did was to walk over and slug Lefty.

Had it not been for Lanning, Lefty would have struck back. Already furious at the shortstop, he would have lost all restraint and gone at it with Bell. He knew he had spiked the third baseman, but not intentionally.

When order was restored—Roughneck fans started to come on the field, and a riot was barely averted—Bell and the third sacker went out of the game. Jackie Kent, following Casey at bat, poled a long single, and two runs came over. Beaumont took the game, 5-4, and of course the league championship as well.

"To heck with them bum Sports!" Tad crowed in the clubhouse. "We won the flag, an' now for that-there Dixie Series!"

Such was the general feeling on the club. The spiking incident had left bad blood between Roughnecks and Sports, but no one on Whitey's squad felt that the blame was on their side. They had seen Lefty get the hip at second, even if the umpire did not, and couldn't blame him if he went into third, spikes high.

News came over the clubhouse radio that the Atlanta Crackers had won the Southern Association play-offs. So it was Beaumont and Atlanta in the Dixie Series.

Lefty rapidly forgot the spiking mishap. He was to get violent reminders of it, however, in the coming Cracker games.

The series was scheduled to open at Atlanta with two games. Then the clubs would return to Beaumont for three contests. If neither team had copped four of the first five, the show would be finished in two games, if necessary, at Ponce de Leon Park in Atlanta.

En route to Atlanta by Pullman, Whitey and Ol' Hoss entertained with tales of the old days.

"I 'member the time I was breakin' in at Waterloo in the Three-I League," Whitey chuckled. "One day we had a runner on third, an' Clyde Swett —he was coachin' at third—he asks the other third baseman to toss him the ball. He wanted a look at it, he said. Nobody called time, so when the busher tosses the ball to Clyde, why, Clyde jumps aside an' lets it roll to the stands. Time they get the darn thing back, our boy on third has scored!"

Hoss chuckled and sucked on his briar. He tried never to let anyone top him with an anecdote; so everyone knew he would follow Whitey's story with one of his own.

"When I was pitchin' for the Indians," he said, "I saw a play somethin' like that one, only better.

Someone hit a double offa me—very seldom they done that, ya know—an' my shortstop took the throw-in from the outfield."

Hoss wheezed and gave the pipe an extra long pull.

"That shortstop was a clever one. He walks over to the runner on second an' tells him to step off the bag, so's he can kick it straight. Minute the runner steps off, the shortstop tags him out."

There was a brief pause, while Hoss beamed and waited for expressions of approval. Then someone asked irreverently, "What's that prove, Hoss?"

Hoss glared and removed his pipe. "It proves," he thundered, "that it never paid nobody to hit a double off the ol' Hoss!"

Ponce de Leon Park, with a capacity of nearly fifteen thousand, overflowed with fans long before game time. In an attempt to salt away the opener, Whitey chose Vic Sedgman to hurl.

"We'll handle one game at a time," Whitey said. "If we take this one, we got 'em on the run first thing."

Cracker manager Will Garber, evidently not wanting to play an ace against an ace, nominated Cry-Baby Schultz, one of his second-string pitchers. Cry-Baby got his nickname from the fact that when he protested an umpire's decision, his round, fat face screwed up like a baby's, and the chunky hurler seemed about to shed tears. Tad knew him well, having played against him several years before.

"Cry-Baby not only squawks on 'bout every pitch," Tad said, "he takes forever to deliver the ball. Garber must figger he'll tire us out from waitin'. It'll be a long game!"

It was a long game. Cry-Baby seemed to count up to sixty before every pitch, and he had endless conferences with his catcher, Buster Brace. The contest was still scoreless going into the eighth. Then Beaumont got a run by bunting Ralph Cavello around to third. Bobby brought him in with another squeeze bunt.

In the last of the ninth, however, the roof caved in on the Roughnecks. Stretch Delaney hit a home run over the left field fence with Luke Smith on base. That clout broke up the ball game, for a 2-1 Cracker victory.

Having won on his gamble with Schultz, a right-hander, Garber came back in the second game next day with his ace southpaw, Bubba Jones. It was good strategy, since Beaumont was loaded with right-handed batters. Lefty and Ralph Cavello were the only two regulars who swung from the port side. Whitey countered with Fritz Obler.

Obler was in trouble from the start. But Roughneck batters, surprisingly enough, found Jones's slants to their liking. The lead see-sawed through the sixth, with first one team ahead by a run, and then the other. In the sixth, Whitey yanked Obler when the latter got in a jam with two down, and sent in his top relief man, Barnacle Bill Berry.

Fifteen Thousand Rabbits' Feet

Berry was just what the doctor ordered. He stopped the Crackers cold. Maxie Schwartz's home run in the eighth with the sacks empty tied the score at six-all.

Meanwhile the Atlanta fans were doing a merciless job of razzing Berry. Barnacle Bill was living up to his reputation as the most superstitious player in the Texas League. Since he would never walk to the mound from the left-hand side of home plate, where the visitors' dugout stood, he had to take a wide detour every inning. Also, after he used the rosin bag, he carefully placed it on the grass about one foot back of the edge of the dirt. One foot. No more, no less.

"He won't go to the box from the left of home," Whitey explained to a reporter, "because the year he led the Texas League with twenty-five wins, he walked on from the right. Says that's what kept his victory string alive. Been doin' it ever since. He'll never change."

In the ninth, after Atlanta failed to score, Bubba Jones seemed to get back his stuff. He struck out Gates and got Art Gray on a foul fly. Then Lefty, hitless all day after two singles in the opener, blasted a double into right center. He had to leg it to second, and in the slide his spikes ripped the stockings of Morrie Rosenbaum, the second baseman.

Morrie wasn't sore. He knew it was an accident, the hazard he faced on every similar play. His leg did not even bleed. But with the fans it was different. They poured abuse upon Lefty, screaming that his Texas League tactics would not get by here.

Lefty calmly brushed himself off, the tumult died down, and Casey stepped to the plate.

With two out, Casey had to hit. Bubba pitched carefully, trying to get the hitter on bad balls. Apparently the plan was to issue a pass if Casey would not bite at poor serves. The pass came, putting another runner on, but giving the infield a chance for a force play at second.

As Jackie Kent came up, he tugged at his cap. It was the signal for the hit-and-run. Just before he stepped into the batter's box, he touched his visor again. That meant he would hit on the second pitch.

Lanning, coaching at third, cupped his hands and shouted, "Over the fence, kid! Blast one, Jackie boy!"

Bubba worked cagily. He gave Jackie one high and wide, hoping to pull him off balance. The umpire called it a strike. Jackie protested loudly, although he would not have tried to hit anyway. But he did not want Bubba to guess that fact.

Lefty eyed Casey on first. Casey returned a meaningful glance.

With Bubba's windup they were off. If the pitch was bad, Jackie could foul it off. If he missed, there was still a chance for the double steal. The Crackers were on edge and had to be kept that way.

Jackie hit the low curve to right. Without his

start, Lefty could not have hoped to score. As it was, it would be close—perilously close.

He high-tailed it straight for home. Out of the corner of his eye, he saw the throw coming in, fast and low, from right field. He crashed into Brace's shin guards as hard as he could.

Brace tagged Lefty's foot and then stepped all over him in the attempt to get Casey at third. Brace got neither man. The plate umpire's palms went down; so did his mate's at third. Jackie ended up on second.

Ralph Cavello skied out to left. Nevertheless, the Roughnecks led by a run, 7-6, going into the last of the ninth. Hold 'em, gang!

Despite the wild clamor of the mob, the jockeying of Cracker subs on the bench, and the bats of Atlanta regulars, Barnacle Bill refused to get jittery. He detoured around home plate to the mound. He used and carefully placed down the rosin bag. He nursed the ball on every throw. The result was that he struck out two batters and forced the third to pop out to Bobby at short. The Roughnecks had the second game, and the series was all even.

Three games coming up in Stuart Stadium. Hey, guys, we can wrap up this thing at home! Take all three games and we've got the series. Waddya say?

Whitey smiled at their enthusiasm.

"One thing at a time, kids," he warned. "We get one day's rest, then Huck Renaldi starts the opener at home. Vic, you'll go in the fourth game. An' I think I'll follow up with the Deacon in the fifth. If we have to go back to Atlanta—" He shrugged his shoulders. "We'll take care of that when the time comes."

Whitey's caution was justified. You don't knock off a well-balanced team like the Crackers in four straight games. Not very often. No, sir!

The gang started off well, though. Lefty won the first game for Huck Renaldi at Stuart Stadium with a homer in the eighth. But he lost the next by throwing over Jackie's head trying to cut down a runner going from first to third. The runner scored, and Vic Sedgman dropped a 1-0 heartbreaker for his second series defeat. Writers tabbed Vic the hard-luck hurler of this post-season classic.

Deacon Dodge fared poorly in the fifth game. The Roughnecks were behind, 6-2, when Barnacle Bill relieved Dodge in the seventh. Bill gave up only one hit, but the Crackers had an easy 6-3 victory.

So it was back to Ponce de Leon Park. Another day off, then up for the sixth game, trailing two games to three. We gotta win this one, guys. Heck, we can do it! Who's gonna pitch?

"I'm startin' Vic again," Whitey said. "He musta run out his string of hard luck by now. He'll win tomorrow. Barnacle Bill will pitch the seventh game, if—"

What he meant by "if" was plain enough.

Fifteen Thousand Rabbits' Feet

Privately Whitey told his coaches, "I gotta give Sedgman another start. If he comes back to us next year with two series defeats an' no wins, I'll have a sorehead on my hands. I gotta make sure he gets one more chance. He's mad enough over Lefty's bad throw as it is."

Lefty made it up to the Beaumont glamour boy in the sixth game. Sedgman, full of courage and determined to annex a series victory, allowed only two hits in nine innings. Meanwhile Lefty thumped two clothesline doubles with men on the sacks each time to give Sedgman a 4-0 shutout. The series was tied up tighter than a drum again.

Even without any publicity shenanigans, the final game had enough importance and interest to fill the Crackers' park several times over. But, as soon as Atlanta's big brass learned that Barnacle Bill would pitch the crucial game, they came up with a brainstorm. It certainly was a lulu.

They purchased fifteen thousand rabbits' feet—all left hind feet, naturally—and promised to distribute them to the fans at the game. Purpose of the charms was to put the hex on Barnacle Bill, whom Leslie Stone of the Atlanta *Constitution* said had "more superstitions than a witch doctor."

"If we put the whammy on Berry," Stone wrote, "the game and the series are ours. Sedgman pitched yesterday. Huck Renaldi can never beat us again. And no other Roughneck pitcher could win."

Sound and whipped-up fury poured down on the

Roughnecks when they took the field for drill next day. Fifteen thousand fans, packed in like sardines, waved fifteen thousand rabbits' feet in their direction. Target of their attack was Barnacle Bill, warming up on the sidelines. But all of the Roughnecks got a going-over. Unsavory remarks were made particularly about Lefty's base-running technique.

"Keep them spikes down, Tarbin," one gravel-voiced partisan shouted, "or you'll get worse than a rabbit's foot!"

"Yeah," came back another, "you'll find a Cracker hot-foot in your teeth!"

Barnacle Bill showed little interest in the riding he took. A diamond-wise veteran, crafty and calm, he waited quietly for the game to open.

Presently the umpire called the managers to the plate, took the opening lineups, adjusted his chest protector, and called in a fog-horn voice, "Puh-lay ball!"

Joe Gates grounded out to short. Art Gray beat out an infield hot shot that the third sacker knocked down but could not handle. Then Lefty caught hold of an outside pitch and sent it sizzling to the shortstop side of second.

It looked like a certain hit. The horsehide skimmed across the infield dirt, headed for center field. Then, seemingly from nowhere, the Cracker shortfielder streaked over, stuck out his glove, and speared the grasscutter. Flip to second, Art Gray

Fifteen Thousand Rabbits' Feet

out by a hair. Pivot by Morrie Rosenbaum, a perfect peg to Stretch Delaney, a double play. Up jerked the base official's thumb. Had there been a roof of solid iron over Ponce de Leon Park, the jubilant Cracker fans would have blown it completely off.

The Roughneck fielders trotted out to their positions. Maxie Schwartz lumbered toward home plate, slapping his mask against his thigh. Barnacle Bill ambled slowly around in back of Maxie and the plate as fifteen thousand wolves howled for his blood.

Not a Cracker reached first base that inning.

As the game went on, it began to look as though no one would ever score. The Crackers got two singles against Berry, while Beaumont hitters managed a double, a long single, and a scratch hit off Big Herman Koch, Atlanta's ace left-hander.

"Them rabbits' feet ain't hurt Bill much yet," a rookie offered in the dugout.

"Shut up!" Ol' Hoss whispered fiercely. "You wanna put the whammy on him?"

Catastrophe struck in the sixth. With one out, Buster Brace slashed a double into left. Big Herman promptly bunted, and Brace came into third with the force of an overloaded freight.

Maxie leaped on top of the ball. Passing up the play at first, he fired to Jackie, who took Brace's assault like a hound dog facing a grizzly. Atlanta's baby blimp landed his bonecrusher form on the bag and Jackie. The third sacker gamely made the tag and tried to hang on. But the crash was too much. Jackie tumbled over backward, dropped the ball, and lay still.

After a time he seemed to be all right. But when he tried to take the ball from Barnacle Bill, who had rushed over to keep Brace from scoring, he groaned.

"My finger! I can't bend it."

The trainer came out, looked at the finger, and shook his head. "I think it's busted. Have to take X-rays."

Jackie protested. He wanted to stay in the game. But after trying a practice throw, he bent his head and sobbed, "I can't throw. It hurts like blazes."

Whitey sent Tad in to play third.

Meanwhile Big Herman had taken second. With one out and men on second and third, Atlanta had the Roughnecks in a spot. They were in still deeper when, after the next Cracker struck out, Morrie Rosenbaum singled both runners home. Stretch Delaney flied out. But the score now was Crackers 2, Beaumont 0.

The Roughnecks dented the plate for the first time in the seventh. Ralph Cavello doubled with one out, took third on Bobby's infield grounder to second, and scored on Maxie's single.

But Atlanta came back with one more in their half. Rough Nelson and Puddinhead Frost opened with bloopers into left. Red Sails sacrificed them

Fifteen Thousand Rabbits' Feet

to third and second, from where, after another out, Nelson alone scored on Brace's scratch single. Big Herman fanned, leaving the Crackers with a 3 to 1 lead.

Neither team added any score in the eighth.

We gotta tie it up! We gotta get two runs, Lefty told himself over and over as the Roughnecks came in after the eighth. One inning to do it!

Art Gray led off and Big Herman tried to push him away from the plate with a duster. The wolves in the stands cheered. Big Herman came in with another close pitch. Art tried to get out of the way, but the fast ball plunked him on the shoulder.

Whitey and several other Roughnecks tumbled angrily from the dugout. Rubbing his shoulder, Art tossed away his bat and jogged down the baseline. The fans booed the Roughnecks and cheered Big Herman. Whitey and the others returned to the bench.

Lefty came out of the on-deck circle. He picked up some dirt, rubbed it in his palms, and settled himself at the plate.

He hadn't even got a loud foul yet off Big Herman. The guy had a fast ball, a sharp curve, and a good change-up. What more could you ask?

Herman's fireball came blazing in. Lefty swung late and fouled. The next offering was a curve, and he missed it by a foot. Herman grinned. The wolves yammered in the stands.

Herman teased him with two wide ones. Two

and two now. The big oaf would not let it get to three and two, because the last pitch would then have to be too good. Lefty had missed a low-breaking curve before. Chances were he'd get that same pitch again now.

He watched it come roaring in. A foot from the plate, it dropped out and down. Lefty sought to avoid swinging too soon; the numerous times he had done so, and sliced the ball, flashed through his mind. Then he was into his swing.

He knew it was solid as soon as he connected. Still, despite his caution, he had undercut a little. His intention was to unload a clothesline smash into the far outfield. But the long ball, travelling with the speed of a bazooka rocket, had too much height. Would it clear the barrier, or fall into Luke Smith's paws in center?

The sphere kept climbing. Yet it moved farther and farther into the deep pasture, too. Lefty rounded first, saw Art still pawing the baseline, hesitating, two thirds of the way to second. He kept his eyes on Art.

Then he saw Art wave his arms, yell, and head for third. Lefty kept running, looking again for the ball. It was just disappearing among the high trees outside the park. Beaumont 3, Crackers 3.

The score stayed knotted through the ninth, tenth, and eleventh. Then, opening the twelfth, Tad cagily worked Big Herman for a pass. Maxie bunted him to second. Sedgman followed with

Fifteen Thousand Rabbits' Feet

another bunt that advanced Tad to the hot corner. Joe Gates hit a blooper to left that scored Tad. Joe was thrown out trying to steal second.

A Cracker fan tried to help his team. As Barnacle Bill took his familiar detour to the mound, the fan jumped from the third-base stands, ran to the mound before he could be halted, and deposited a black tomcat there. The tom arched his back, snarling and spitting as Bill tried to pick him up. Then suddenly the animal turned and raced off the field.

The Crackers made a gallant come-back try. But the more the fans yelled and waved their left hind rabbits' feet, the sharper Barnacle Bill seemed to get. Puddinhead Frost struck out. Casey hauled down Red Sails' long fly. Skeeter Mills drove a hit just inside first base that Lefty could not stab. Buster Brace eked out a pass, although Maxie Schwartz protested so loud and so long on ball four that he nearly got the heave-ho.

The park was a bedlam by the time play was resumed. Lefty felt the tenseness that gripped the entire Roughneck squad. All, that is, except Barnacle Bill. He appeared almost to toy with Handy Hale, pinch hitting for Big Herman. After two strikes and three balls, which seemed to Lefty an eternity in coming, Handy flied out to Art Gray.

The Roughnecks stormed into the locker room, noisy and jubilant. Tad Reno kissed Casey. Whitey hugged Art for his final putout catch. Everyone yelled and danced like a wild Indian. Joe Gates punctuated the noise now and again with his repeated "Yippay!" Hot steam filled the shower room, and the warm moisture of it went deep into Lefty's lungs as he showered, along with the biting smell of liniment and the stale odor of sweat.

Barnacle Bill, naked to the waist and with perspiration streaming down his body, was surrounded at his locker by reporters.

"How did you feel out there today?" someone asked. "Especially with those fifteen thousand rabbits' feet waving at you all the time."

"You can quote me as saying," Bill remarked with deliberation, "that I never even turned a hare!"

CHAPTER XII

OUT OF THE TIGER CHAIN

SOME of the Roughnecks left immediately for their homes after the series, without making the return trip to Beaumont. Bobby Dale caught a train for New York en route to Maine. Art purchased a green convertible in Atlanta and set off on the drive to Chicago, taking Ralph Cavello and Casey along. Joe Gates' home was only about fifty miles from Atlanta, and his folks, who had come in for the Atlanta games, were driving him home.

"What you doing this winter?" Bobby asked Lefty, before he took the train. "Why not come with me to Maine?"

Lefty hunched his shoulders and pretended to shiver. "I'll pass up those Northern winters, thanks, Bobby. I'm allergic to snow and ice. First I'm going back to Beaumont, and from there—well, I don't know."

Later, back at his hotel in Beaumont, he found a message asking him to call Mark Ritter, sports editor of the Beaumont *Star*. He assumed that Mark wanted an interview on the series. Why didn't he contact Whitey, or some of the other players who were in the city for another day or two?

He waited until after lunch to phone the *Star*. Ritter himself answered.

"Hello, Lefty. Congratulations to all the Roughnecks on winning the series. How does it feel to be on a championship club?"

"Great!" Lefty said. "Just great, Mark."

"You did a lot to make it possible, Lefty."

"Thanks. I also came near cooking our goose more than once. I'll never forgive myself for losing that fourth game for Vic."

"Forget it, kid. Everyone makes errors. Remember the Snodgrass muff? It's all in the game."

"What did you want to talk to me about, Mark?"

There was a pause on the other end of the line, and Lefty could faintly hear Ritter's voice giving directions to a reporter. Then the editor spoke into the mouthpiece again.

"Ever done any writing, Lefty?"

Lefty hesitated, surprised. "Why, just in my courses at school. I've never done much else along that line."

"Well, you're a college man. You ought to be able to write some, at least. Here's the set-up. Pat Long—he covers schoolboy basketball for us—just had an operation. He wants to take a long rest, and plans to stay off the job until maybe February. You know anything about basketball?"

"Why, sure. I played in prep school, and a little at Bolton."

"Swell. Would you consider filling in for Pat

Out of the Tiger Chain

until he comes back? That is, unless you have some other plans."

Lefty thought fast. He had intended going to Oregon for a week or two, and then spending the rest of the winter in Florida. There were ballplayers there all winter, and by talking with them and working out occasionally he would have that much of a jump on the others when spring training began. However, Mark's offer sounded interesting. A little experience as a scribe might be good. Help him to see athletes from the writer's viewpoint. When his playing days were over, who knows? He might become a baseball writer, like Don Carlson of Tulsa, who once had been a professional ball player.

He made up his mind. "Gee, Mark, thanks. I'd be glad to take the job. That's if you think you can put up with a rank amateur."

Mark's soft laugh came over the wire, above the background clatter of typewriter keys. "I think you'll do, kid."

He met Whitey in the lobby a few minutes later and told him about the new job. The manager laughed. "Probably the schoolboys won't be as tough on you as us pros are on the writin' guys."

"I hope not."

Whitey explained that he was remaining in Beaumont until the major league meetings at New York in December.

"A lot of plannin' to do for next year," he said.

"No news yet, but there'll be changes, of course. Different faces at spring trainin'. Some old ones gone up in the chain, others sent down the river."

"No dope on that yet, I suppose." Lefty was thinking about his own chances for next year, and Art's, and Bobby's, and the outlook for Jackie Kent and scrappy Joe Gates. He knew that all of them, except possibly Bobby, had their hearts set on playing in the big show.

Whitey shook his head. "Only thing I can say is that Tad is quittin' as a player. But he'll be back next year to coach the hitters. I've never seen a man who knows more about hittin' than Tad does. He's a master of the art."

They shook hands. "I'll be back here right after Christmas," Whitey said. "Drop around an' see me."

Beaumont, like all of Texas, was a hotbed of basketball. Even in the fall, before football had faded out, Lefty got a chance to write about the court game. During the early weeks on his new job, he spent most of the time talking with high school coaches and players. Mark Ritter and some of the other *Star* men gave him tips on writing sports. By early December he was ready, and his accounts of the games were straightforward and clear.

His most exciting night was at an out-of-the-city gym, when a boy, becoming confused in a contest that went into the last second still tied, threw the ball into the wrong basket and won the game for the other team.

The city room was still chuckling about the incident late that night. Lefty had just got in and typed his story for the morning edition. Suddenly a man at the teletype machine yelled, "Hey, boys, c'mere!"

Everyone knew something big was coming over the wire. Lefty gave his last sheet to the copy boy and sauntered over. Probably some big news had broken in Washington, or there had been a bad accident, an airplane crash or something—

A reporter was reading off the story aloud.

"In the biggest deal of this week's major league meetings, which closed tonight at the Hotel Astoria, Detroit, New York, and Chicago pulled off a three-cornered American League trade that will have the baseball world talking all winter. Six players are involved in the big swap, including Sambo Kellogg, home-run hitting star of the Yankees. Here is how the thing lines up:

"The Yankees sent Kellogg and Bat Kirby, utility infielder, to the White Sox for pitcher Paul Brennan, a twenty-game winner last year. Chicago then traded Kirby and first-baseman Johnny (the Czech) Marsak to the Tigers for outfielders Noodles Noonan and Johnny Gerro. This solidifies the Chicago outfield for next season."

Someone hanging over the teletype whistled. "It

sure does!" he said. "What an outfield Chicago will have next year!"

"Shut up!" another reporter grumbled. "There's more."

The man who was reading off the wire went on: "Meanwhile, the Tigers bought veteran outfielder Indian Bob Pratt from the Richmond Virginians. But in order to get Pratt, a hard hitter who will help make up for the departure of Noonan and Gerro, Detroit had to send a good hitter to the Virginians. They did it by selling outright to Richmond the contract of their slugging first baseman at Beaumont in the Texas League, Lefty Bruce Tarbin, who batted .320 over the regular season. This big deal gives the Tigers—"

A whoop rose in the city room, engulfing the droning voice of the reader. Lefty stood, dazed, amidst the clamor. He could hardly believe that the news was true, that he had been sold out of the Tiger chain, outright to another club. Why had they let him go? Had Whitey okayed the deal?

The soft voice of Mark Ritter was at his elbow.

"We'll hate to lose you, Lefty. Sorry to see you drop from the Tiger organization, too. But the Virginians are a triple-A club, and it's really a promotion for you."

Lefty wondered. He had been moving along in the well-oiled machinery of a big-league outfit. His chances for eventual promotion to the parent Tigers had looked good. Now, in a strange set-up, forced to make good all over again—well, was it a lucky break or a bad one?

Mark made him feel a little better. "Now that the Tigers have Marsak, they won't need a first sacker for a long time. Marsak's only about twenty-five years old. So you would have a tough time trying to break into the Detroit lineup. Now, if you make good at Richmond, they can sell you to the highest bidder. That means a rich team and probably a good one."

"Yeah," Lefty said. "Sure."

He felt better after he thought it over. The move would take him from double-A to triple-A ball, into the International League. If he made good with Richmond, it was, as Mark pointed out, only one step higher to the majors. The Virginians could sell him to the highest bidder. That might be good. In the meantime, it was Lefty's job to click in triple-A.

He could hardly wait for Christmas to come and go, so that he could talk with Whitey. He wanted to get the first-hand story on the deal. Had the Tigers soured on him, and taken Marsak in order to get rid of Tarbin? Could be. Lefty knew his fielding was not the best.

On the other hand, he knew also that in order to swing a major deal, any club has to let go of players it would rather keep. The Yankees never parted willingly with Sambo Kellogg's big bat. Not by a long shot. But unless New York improved its pitching, there would be no pennant at Yankee Stadium the following year. So they traded Kellogg to get Paul Brennan.

With Lefty still a year or two away, maybe the Tigers figured that to be contenders next season, they had to strengthen their infield. They tried three first basemen last year, Lefty remembered. The ones who could hit could not field. The good fielders couldn't hit the size of their hats.

When Lefty walked into the Roughneck office three days after Christmas, Whitey was there. The manager smiled warmly at his ex-first baseman as they shook hands.

"Sit down, Lefty. How've ya been? How did things go up there in the press box?"

"Swell. How did things go at the Hotel Astoria?"

Whitey smiled as he caught the meaning. "I hated to let you go," he said quietly. "Tried to get Richmond to go for Tom Silk instead. But the Orioles have strings on Silk and wouldn't give him up. Finally I had to give in. Couldn't stop 'em anyway. I'm just a little shot in the Tiger set-up, you know."

"I think some day you will be a big shot, Whitey. That's one reason I wanted to stay with Detroit."

"Thanks, Lefty. But let me give you some advice. Take this deal as a big chance to move ahead. Richmond's manager, Denny Moss, is a swell guy. I played ball with him on the Coast. Make good in the International League, an'—well, you know what I mean!"

Out of the Tiger Chain

Lefty could not wait for his sports writing days to end and spring training to start. In mid-January Pat Long decided to resume his newspaper job. Lefty promptly went to Sarasota and looked up Pete Travers at the Vista Hotel, where he took a room.

A letter post-marked Richmond finally caught up with him there. It was his contract with the Virginians. Enclosed was a letter welcoming him to the club and instructing him to report for spring training at Sanford on March 15. The contract called for a sizeable raise over his Beaumont salary, so he quickly signed it, mailed it back, and settled down to await the beginning of practice.

One other thing of interest broke into his Florida vacation. It was an A.P. sports item from Beaumont, dealing with the Roughnecks. The despatch stated that Art Gray had been sold to the Kansas City Blues, a Yankee farm. Bobby Dale and Joe Gates were moved up to Seattle of the Pacific Coast League. They still were Tiger property. And two Beaumont pitchers, Vic Sedgman and Barnacle Bill Berry, had been called up for a spring tryout with the Tigers.

"I hope they all make it," Lefty said with sincerity to Pete.

The oldster grinned. "Maybe some day all of yuh will be playin' against each other in the majors. That'll be the day!"

CHAPTER XIII

ACTION AT PARKER FIELD

"It's great to be a Virginian!"

Such was the feeling on the Richmond club, and after one day in camp Lefty saw why. Most of the players were young and eager to make the grade. Their attitude was that this was their big chance, and not one of them intended to fail.

And that was Lefty's viewpoint, also. To him, only one place was the satisfactory one to play ball —the major leagues. But no matter where he was, he gave everything he had. He intended always to perform that way.

Chief Reynolds, Richmond coach, explained things to him. "The experts ain't planning on us havin' a big season. They say we don't have enough hittin', fieldin', or pitchin'. Wal, mebbe so. But we're full up with good, healthy youngsters. They're

Action at Parker Field

a fighting gang, an' that's what we want. That's the kind of club we're tryin' to build here. If we hadn't lost Indian Bob Pratt, though, things might look better."

Lefty winced. Reynolds probably meant nothing personal by his remark about Pratt. Everyone knew, however, that the Virginians would miss Indian Bob's war club. There was little faith that the rookie from Beaumont would clout the ball like Pratt.

One thing was sure. The team needed a first sacker. Rich in outfielders, the club without Lefty would have been forced to convert an outer gardener into a first baseman.

"Matter of fact, I plan to keep an extra outfielder for first-base insurance," manager Denny Moss said. "He'll have to be a good fielder, though, because ground balls goin' through first base is what has made my hair gray. See?" He doffed his cap and showed his completely silver thatch.

For the time, Lefty had no trouble nailing down the first-base job. There just wasn't any real competition. He realized now why the Virginians had let their star outfielder Indian Bob go on condition that they could buy a first baseman. What worried him was, could he hit enough to take up the slack left by Pratt's departure?

He got his first real chance to show his stuff in a grapefruit league tilt with the Cardinals at Clearwater. The field was rough, and he had some trouble with ground balls. At bat he rapped a single off Ken James, but went hitless his other three trips.

In the locker room he overheard Pete Clark mumbling to Derek Bannhoff.

"Can't figure that screwy deal," Clark was saying. "We're all glad to see Bob go up to the majors, sure. But this guy Tarbin—over the season, I bet he don't hit his weight!"

As the training grind drew to an end, Clark's prediction looked good. Lefty could not find his batting eye. He never had encountered much trouble hitting in the spring, since batters are usually ahead of the hurlers in pre-season games. But were pitchers up here in faster company going to be too much for him?

Richmond opened the season at home in Parker Field against Rochester. The Red Wings, weakest hitting team in the league the year before, took two of the three games. Lefty got two singles in ten trips.

"Your fieldin' at least is better'n we expected to have before you came," Chief Reynolds grunted. "Never mind 'bout the hittin'. You look good an' loose up there. Time comes, you'll break out. Wait an' see."

He was thankful for Reynolds' encouragement. But the following three games with Toronto did not help any. The Maple Leafs also won two out of three. Then the Virginians dropped the first two contests with Ottawa's Athletics; and on a damp,

Action at Parker Field

overcast day, they came into the last game of the home stand with only two victories against six defeats. Their average was .250, and they were in seventh place in the league. Lefty was batting only .189. The future looked bleak.

Although none of the Virginians said a word about it, Lefty had the uncomfortable feeling that they resented his failure to hit. The ghost of Indian Bob haunted him more than ever. Or the ghost of Indian Bob's war club, at least.

That final day of the home stand they faced Ottawa's Hy Bridges, veteran fastball artist. Everyone knew the visitors were starting Bridges because the day was murky and the Virginians wouldn't be able to see Hy's fireball.

Though at first Bridges made the experts look good, hurling no-hit ball going into the fifth, the Athletics themselves could do little with Jocko Jones. They got only two singles off Jones through the fifth. In the last of that inning, with one out, the fleet-footed Cuban center fielder of the Virginians, Luis Montos, worked Bridges for a pass. Hod Miller, batting just before Lefty, struck out. Luis streaked for second on the last pitch and slid safely under the catcher's throw.

Pint-sized Eddie Hanley, at second for the Athletics, was furious at the call. He stood chest to chest with umpire Bucky Hirst, jawing angrily, kicking dirt over the arbiter's shoes. Hirst lifted his shoulders, turned on his heel, and walked back toward second base. Finally Hanley shut up and took his position. The fans and the Virginians on the bench razzed him mercilessly.

Lefty came out of the on-deck circle, waving two bats. Two outs. This was the time for a hit. If he could bring Luis in, the run might mean the ball game. He junked one bat, rubbed his palms dry on his uniform, pressed his cleats into the dirt, and waited for the pitch.

It came in, fast and close. Strike one. Normally Lefty would have snapped at it. But as the ball came roaring in, a particle of dust flew into his eye. Instinctively he drew back from the close pitch. He called time and wiped his watery eye.

He heard Eddie Hanley at second yell, "Stand up to the plate, you bum!"

He said nothing, but his mates in the dugout took up the argument for him. They shrieked insults at Hanley, and pounded on the dugout railing with their bats. The tension crept into the stands, and furious roars from the home fans beat down upon the field.

"Shut up, Hanley!"

"You fresh busher!"

"Send the lousy little so-and-so back to Ottawa!"

The umpires gazed stolidly at the plate, Hanley hitched at his belt, meanwhile yelling something unintelligible, and Lefty stepped back to the plate.

Two strikes, no balls. He would not get another good pitch right away. Irritated in spite of himself by Hanley's taunts, he determined to cream the first pitch if it was in there. At second, Luis Montos kicked the dirt with his spikes and waited.

Bridges put one in high and outside. It was too wide to get the fat of the wood on. But it hung for a second out there. Lefty uncoiled his stick, giving his wrist a quick snap as ash met horsehide. He caught the pitch and sent it, a flying white streak, over the shortstop's head.

It was one of the old-time clothesline hits, Lefty's first as a Virginian. Gloating, he watched it out of the corner of his eye as he roared into first base, hearing Chief Reynolds' high-pitched yell: "Take two! Take two!"

He saw the ball keep its height, not more than twelve feet off the ground. It continued on, sank a little, hit the fence several feet from the ground, and rebounded directly into the center fielder's mitt.

Lefty's twinkling hoofs churned up the dirt. He knew Luis would score easily, but the play at second had to be eyelash close. He watched the ball come in on a line, hit the ground, rush straight for Eddie Hanley's waiting glove. Lefty took off in a high, charging slide.

Stubbornly, Eddie tried to force him to go around the bag. But after Hanley's taunts, Lefty was in no mood to go chicken. He had the right of way on the basepath, and he was going to take it. He went in with spikes flashing.

He felt the sharp steel rake across Eddie's leg, ripping open the stocking. Eddie fell as he was about to make the tag, but he came up fast, swinging the ball in his meat hand as he did so. He tagged Lefty hard across the mouth, a tooth-jarring sock that made everything dissolve in Lefty's mind except cold, relentless hatred for the cocky little second sacker.

He came up, fists pumping. The ball flew out of Hanley's grasp and the little guy threw a fast punch. One thing, Eddie wasn't yellow. Then Lefty caught him in the brisket, dropped a left to the stomach, and finished the brief fight with a hard right to the jaw.

It took the full detail of Richmond police to prevent a riot. The fans luckily were kept off the field. Lefty found himself trading punches with the rest of Ottawa's infield for a moment, until the Virginians rushed in. After several minutes of wild confusion, cooler heads pried the fighters apart.

Lefty was safe at second, but he and Eddie were thrown out of the game. Lefty showered and waited at his locker for the boys to troop in. Pete Clark was first, and he came over to shake Lefty's hand.

"We shut 'em out, 2-0, kid," Pete said. "And lemme tell yuh, that Hanley got just what he was askin' for."

The others, coming in, backed up Pete's words.

Two days later the Virginians opened their first road trip at Syracuse. The evening before the game, in his Syracuse hotel room, Lefty got the news he was waiting for.

"You've been suspended for ten days," Denny

Action at Parker Field

told him. "Same for Hanley. I hate to lose you for that time, Lefty. But seein' Hanley get his was almost worth it."

Chief Reynolds had come in with Denny. The Chief bit off a piece of plug tobacco and said, with a twinkle in his eyes, "You gotta learn to control that temper, kid. It'll keep you in hot water all the time. Don't let it happen again!"

Then he shoved his cud into the side of his mouth and went on: "I mean, don't let any jerk try to get away with that kinda stuff, ever. Else they'll run yuh outta this-here man's game!"

At Syracuse, Buffalo, and Rochester, Lefty rode out his suspension in the dressing room. He heard the games over a portable radio. Surprisingly, the battle with Hanley seemed to light a spark in the Virginians' play. Leaving home with a three-six record, they came to life on the road. They began to hit, fielded like crazy, and swept the three-game Syracuse series. They took three of four at Buffalo, two of three at Rochester, and then got aboard the train for Toronto. Their won-lost record was eleven and eight. It brought them from seventh place to fourth.

At Toronto, Lefty returned to the lineup. The enforced layoff, he found, had affected his batting eye. He got only two singles in the Maple Leaf series. The Canadian fans razzed him for his poor hitting and for the brush at Richmond with Eddie Hanley.

It was in Ottawa, though, that he took the worst

going-over from the fans that he had ever experienced. Hanley was their favorite, the hometown hotshot who could do no wrong. The fact that Lefty was much the larger of the two added to the rooters' bitterness.

Abuse surged down on him during that series in Lansdowne Park. If he was ever going to learn to take it, and come back for more, this surely was his chance. He stayed in the lineup, but his hitting did not improve, and the jockeying began to affect his fielding. The Virginians took only one of four games from the Athletics. Later they broke even in the four contests at Montreal.

He had a talk with Denny on the long ride back to Richmond. The team had dropped into fifth place.

"This club has got the makin's of a pennant winner," Denny said, running his fingers through his gray hair. "As soon as we start clickin', we'll be up there."

"Guess I'm not helping much," Lefty said dejectedly. "I sure haven't made up for Pratt at the plate."

Denny gave him a sharp look.

"So that's what's eatin' ya? Forget it! You've settled our first-base problem, an' with your smooth, easy swing up there at the dish, the ball is bound to start landin' safe. You just haven't got goin' yet. Forget it!"

Rube Bromberg pitched the first game after the

return to Parker Field. Rochester Red Wings provided the opposition. Jeers turned to cheers for Lefty here. The fans took an altogether different view of the Hanley-Tarbin feud than did the Ottawa faithful. Sports editor Charlie Johnson wrote in the *Blade:*

"We don't condone roughneck play on the field. The game of baseball has graduated from those days. But when a Virginian has enough of the old college try to go into second base the way Lefty Tarbin did in the last Ottawa game here, we say: 'More power to him.'

"And when he actually gets mad enough to sock a wise guy who tries to shove the ball down his throat—well, we're going out to watch those Virginians!"

Lefty contributed a double and a single to the Virginian attack behind the Rube. The game went into the last of the ninth tied at 2-2. Then catcher Zeke Mondello, built like a cave man of the Stone Age, lumbered to the plate with two out and a man on first. Zeke promptly hit the first pitch over the fence, and the Virginians copped, 4-2.

Zeke was the last one into the shower room after the winning clout. Pete Clark yelled at him as he came in.

"Nice work, Zeke! Too bad that face of your'n ain't as pretty as the ball looked, goin' over the fence."

Zeke only grunted.

Spirit began to seep into the club. Luis Montos, labelled the Cuban Greyhound, had Pete Clark and the usually low-geared Derek Bannhoff racing after every ball in their section of the outfield. The infielders made almost impossible stops and the zip came back into their throws. Batting averages started to climb. By August, the Virginians were in third place, trailing Ottawa and Syracuse in that order.

"Maybe we won't win the flag," shortstop Mose Myers grunted. "But we're gonna have somethin' to say about who does!"

August rolled by in a long, sultry wave of endless heat. Much as Lefty dreaded facing the barbs of Canadian fans, the weather was much cooler up there off the Lakes. More road trips came and went. Attendance at home climbed, and Richmond approached that state of baseball madness which comes with a pennant contender.

Still, the Virginians could not climb above third place. After Labor Day, the teams came hustling into the final stretch of the dingdong pennant race. Richmond cleaned up a series with the Red Wings, but the Syracuse Chiefs swept theirs against Buffalo. That left two complete series for all three top teams. Ottawa, the leaders, came to Richmond for their season finale after Buffalo. The Chiefs closed at Rochester and Montreal.

Buffalo took one game of the Ottawa series. Syracuse made a clean sweep of Rochester, and the Vir-

Action at Parker Field

ginians whipped the Maple Leafs every game. Ottawa's Athletics now led Syracuse by one game, the Chiefs in turn being a game up on Richmond.

In the first game, the Virginians tripped Ottawa, 2-1, on a nicely pitched game by Rube Bromberg. Syracuse drubbed Montreal, 6-1, and tied for the league lead.

The second Richmond-Athletics game went into extra innings without a score. Then in the eleventh, Ottawa got a man on first with one out. The next batter hit a grasscutter to Lefty's right. He fielded the ball, fumbled momentarily, and then got off an awkward throw to second. He got his man at the keystone, but the return was a shade too late to nip the runner at first.

There should have been three out. But with only two gone, the next Athletic batter tripled to deep left, scoring the man from first. Ottawa hung a heart-breaking 1-0 shutout on the Virginians, shoving them deeper into third place. Syracuse stayed in a tie for the lead with a 4-3 win over the Royals.

"We're out of it," Denny said mournfully. "But we still got a game to play. If we can take Ottawa tomorrow, and the Chiefs win, it's the pennant for Syracuse."

Yes, the Virginians were mathematically out of it. Ordinarily, they might not have had the pep to fight in a game that meant nothing to them on the last day. They were set in third place, and couldn't go higher, no matter what. But perhaps because of the bad blood existing that year between the two teams, or because of a flaming spirit that some of the writers credited to Lefty Tarbin, the players bore down as though they still were after the International League flag. Jocko Jones set the Athletics down with three singles, and Richmond breezed in, 3-0.

"How's Syracuse doin'?" Zeke Mondello wheezed as he pulled off his spikes.

"Wait a minute," Lefty said. "I think the radio has some scores."

The room went silent as the announcer's voice came over the air.

"Some last-minute International League scores: Richmond 3, Ottawa 0. A three-hit shutout for Jocko Jones. Now if the Syracuse Chiefs can take the Royals, that pennant is theirs. No news as yet . . . Wait a minute, folks. Here comes a bulletin. Maybe—yes, this is it. Syracuse 3, Montreal 1 . . . It's the flag for Syracuse!"

From the noise that broke out among the Virginians, you would have thought that they, and not the Chiefs, were going into the Junior World's Series. Pete Clark summed up their real feelings when he said, "You got the pennant this year, Chiefs. But watch out for the Virginians next season!"

CHAPTER XIV

HELLO, FENWAY PARK!

LEFTY skipped the World's Series and left immediately for Florida. He had several invitations to visit during the winter. Art Gray, Bobby Dale, and Joe Gates all wanted to see him and talk stove-league baseball. But the Sunny South was the place where he could best keep in condition for next season's play. Another year in triple-A might get him a bid from the majors. That was something worth working for!

At first he thought of going by way of Beaumont to see Whitey. He still hoped the Tigers might buy him back. Then he decided to let fate shape his course. He would play his fastest ball next season, and hope that the ever-present major league scouts would camp on his trail.

When he reached Pete Travers' place, he found another visitor there. It was Shorty Timmins—bald, round, and jolly as ever.

They fanned for several hours. Finally Shorty said, "Know how come the Virginians got you last year?"

Lefty shook his head.

"It was Chief Reynolds. He saw you in the Cracker series. When Whitey tried to sic Denny Moss onto Tom Silk, Reynolds said no. Denny thinks the Chief is the world's best judge of baseball ivory; so when Reynolds says to take Tarbin, Moss held out for you."

All that winter Lefty wondered whether or not the Chief had done him a favor. If he had stayed in the Tiger chain, he might be going up next year. As it was— Oh, well.

He swam, fished, walked, and after a month's layoff, started throwing a baseball again. His Richmond contract came, and being satisfied with the terms he quickly signed it and returned it. The months slipped by, and then came the call to report at Sanford once more.

Most of the old gang was there. Derek Bannhoff and a relief pitcher had been traded to the Red Wings for Boris Romakov, a hard-hitting outfielder. Pitcher Frankie Bishop was purchased from Syracuse. Of course there was the usual flock of rookies, including two first basemen from lower classifications. Otherwise, there weren't many changes.

"If we don't win that-there flag this year," Zeke Mondello said, "I am goin' inta the movies and play opposite some of them beauty queens."

"A long way opposite, I bet," Pete Clark ob-

Hello, Fenway Park!

served. "Ya mean you're goin' to haunt houses in horror pictures."

Zeke disdained to reply.

Lefty found himself battling Dave Kimball, up from Birmingham, for the first-base slot. Kimball was a good glove man, and if his hitting improved he would make a real bid for Lefty's job. But as yet the smooth-fielding rookie did not have the necessary batting power.

The pennant-hungry Virginians opened the championship schedule at Buffalo. Eddie Hanley now played second for the Bisons, after a winter trade, and the one-time Ottawa man of motion sparked the Buffalo team. But he and Lefty had no trouble during the opening contests. After the four-game Bison get-away, which the teams split, Syracuse came to Parker Field to begin the new Virginian home campaign.

It was a different story from last year, when the stands were scarcely one-quarter full on opening day. This time, with the champion Chiefs as guests, and with a Richmond nine that promised to be a strong contender, nearly fifteen thousand fans stormed the park.

Jocko Jones, who had won the second game at Buffalo, took the mound for the Virginians. Jocko's sinker ball was hot stuff at Parker Field, and Denny Moss wanted to get off on the right foot before Richmond's steamed-up baseball public.

Jocko set down the Chiefs one-two-three in the first inning. Then Luis Montos, opening the Virginians' half, worked Fred Ericson for a pass. It was too early in the game to bunt. So Denny signalled Hod Miller to hit away. But Hod topped a slow roller to the first baseman, who tagged him out. Luis took second.

Lefty, batting third again, dug in at the plate. He had not been bothered much last year by what the writers called Ericson's "southpaw magic." Swinging from the port side as he did, he usually had fair luck with southpaws.

"If he comes in with that slider," Lefty thought grimly, "I ought to be able to rattle it off the fence."

The first pitch was letter-high but close. The catcher faked a throw to second and Luis scurried back to the bag. The catcher walked toward the mound, rubbing up the ball. He walked half way, tossed the ball to Ericson, and came trudging back.

Luis scraped the base path restlessly. Ericson's arm went back, then swung forward and down with almost effortless motion.

The ball came *zing!* down the alley. It headed for Lefty's shoulders, dipping sharply before it crossed the plate. Lefty brought his thick, bony wrists around in a close-to-the-shoulder swing. He caught the pitch early, pulled it hard into right field. The right fielder sprinted for the high-sailing pellet, but it hit against the barrier at the 325-foot mark long before he could reach it. Luis scored and Lefty camped on second.

Richmond could not score again. The Chiefs pushed across the tying run in the sixth with two hits and an error. Going into the ninth, the score remained a 1-1 tie.

Tragedy loomed for the Virginians in the ninth. Jocko Jones raised a blister on his pitching hand. He retired the Chiefs in the ninth, but showed Denny the blister when he came in to the bench.

"We gotta score this half, gang," Denny told them. "We gotta ice the game now. Clark—Myers—Mondello. Get that run!"

Pete Clark flied out. Myers scratched a single through the box, and Zeke's bunt put him on second. It was Jocko's turn to bat, but with the blister he couldn't have swung a Japanese fan. Denny sent in Dave Kimball to hit.

"The kid's new," Denny mumbled. "They won't know how to pitch him." To Kimball he said, "Powder the first thing that looks good, Dave."

Kimball watched two outside balls go by, then grounded weakly to the first baseman. So much for Denny's hunch. To make it worse, the Chiefs scored a run in the tenth. The Virginians could not get it back, and Syracuse walked off with the game, 2-1.

Lefty talked with Denny that evening. As a result, the next morning Lefty and Dave Kimball were on the diamond for hitting practice. For several weeks the two continued the extra workouts.

Slowly Kimball's swing improved. He met the ball more sharply, and some of his drives were on the order of Lefty's clothesline smashes.

"You'll do better," Lefty said confidently. "What you need is that easy, smooth motion. Keep your bat on the level. Don't try to murder the pitch; just punch it out there between the fielders. It doesn't have to go over their heads. Remember—keep your eye on the ball all the time!"

Gratefully Dave thanked him. "Sure hope you don't think I'm a know-it-all," the Birmingham alumnus said, "but I'd like to pay you back a little for all this help."

"Sure, Dave. What is it?"

"I've been watching your fielding, Lefty. I think there's one hitch in it."

"What's that?"

"On a double-play ball, when you make the peg to second, you stand flat-footed. That way, there's less power and speed behind your throw. And it makes you slower getting back to first to finish up the DP."

"What do you think I should do?"

"If you pivot on your right foot, bringing your left one over in a step toward second, you'll get your body behind the throw. The ball will get away faster and move faster. Then you can swing back on your right foot again and get a quick break to cover first when the peg comes back from second."

Hello, Fenway Park!

Lefty gave a thoughtful, "Um-m-m. Maybe you're right. I'll try it. Thanks, Dave."

In the weeks that followed, the Virginians alternated between second and third place in the International League standings. It was clear that Syracuse again was the team to beat, with Richmond and the Montreal Royals as the strongest contenders behind the Chiefs. One day in Montreal, the teams came into the ninth inning in a 3-3 deadlock. Dave Kimball came up to pinch hit for the Virginians with a man on second, and promptly rattled the left-field fence with a 340-foot triple. Then he scored on Hod Miller's single.

Montreal failed to tally in its half, and the Virginians squeezed up into the league's second spot.

Meanwhile Lefty had been working on the first-to-second-and-back double play. Dave's advice was good, and on one occasion Lefty and Mose Myers pulled off a lightning DP that choked off a Syracuse rally and saved the game for Richmond.

Then one day early in June Lefty had a summons from the front office. When he got there, Denny Moss and Chief Reynolds were closeted with the Virginians' head man, Bill Clemson.

"Sit down," Clemson said. "Have a cigar?"

Lefty smiled. "I don't smoke, thanks."

"Good idea. Wish more of my players didn't."

There was a moment's silence. Then Clemson

went on, "I liked the way you knocked off those two Chiefs with that double play last week." He cleared his throat. "There was someone else in my box who liked it, too. Odie Brewster, a Red Sox scout."

Lefty stiffened in his chair. He squirmed a little. What in heck was this all about? What was coming now?

Clemson smiled faintly. "In fact, Brewster made us an offer. It was okayed by the Red Sox owners over the phone last night; so we closed a deal. We've sold you, Lefty. To the Boston Red Sox, for immediate delivery."

As though they were in a storm-pitched boat at sea, the room swam about Lefty. Then, as he looked at the smiling faces and extended hands of Myers and Reynolds, he realized that the news was true.

"You leave on the afternoon plane for Boston," Denny told him. "The Sox play a night game at Fenway Park. You prob'ly won't play tonight, but you can take in part of the game."

Swift thoughts flashed through Lefty's mind. "What happens to their regular first baseman?"

"He isn't hitting, so they're sendin' him out. That Red Sox first-base job is yours. All you have to do is keep it!"

Those last words pounded in his brain as he flew north to Boston. That first-base job is yours—*if you can keep it!* Well, he reflected tightly, I intend to keep it!

Obviously Dave Kimball's improved hitting had

Hello, Fenway Park!

been the factor in causing Clemson and Denny to make the sale. If Dave could hit—and Lefty was sure he would—they would have to make a place for him on the Virginians. Richmond big brass knew Lefty was wild to move up to the big leagues. All around, it was a great deal for everyone. It would be a good deal, too, Lefty vowed, for the Red Sox. In third place behind Chicago and New York, the Sox had plenty of time still to batter their way to the top of the league. Lefty aimed to help them get there.

Ed Bowler, Red Sox general manager, met him at Logan Airport. Bowler, a tall, smiling man, took Lefty's hand in a tight grip as he welcomed him.

"We've heard a lot about you, Lefty," Bowler said in the taxi on the way to Fenway Park, "an' all of it is good. Odie Brewster says you have the makin's of a great first baseman."

Quietly Lefty answered, "I'll sure do my best." He liked the tall, friendly general manager right away.

That night's game was half over when they climbed up to the Fenway press box. Bowler introduced him to the writers, who looked him over carefully. He could tell what they were thinking. *So this is the guy who is going to help the Red Sox win the pennant.*

Down on the field, things were not going so well for Boston. Detroit's Tigers led the Sox in a free-hitting game, 8-4. Unfortunately, the Tigers were doing most of the hitting. This state of affairs did not suit Boston's rabid fans, and they were letting the world know about it.

Otto Luber, the stocky, middle-aged Boston manager, was in the coaching box at first base. A loud fan in one of the box seats incessantly rode Otto, second-guessing him on every play.

Finally, with one out, Tony Maloski of the Sox sliced a single into right. Otto stood in the coach's box, arms on his hips for a moment, staring into the flood-lit outfield. Then suddenly he turned and walked toward the big mouth in the box seat. Up in press row, Lefty could see from Otto's lips what the stocky manager was saying.

"All right, mister," Otto called to the astonished customer. "What'll we do now?"

The fan was taken aback for a moment. But only for a moment. You never find a veteran grandstand manager out of free advice. This one was no exception. He leaned forward eagerly and offered his gem of wisdom for the Red Hose cause.

Of course Lefty could not hear what the fan said. But when Otto turned toward the plate and swung an imaginary bat for the benefit of Johnny Palmer, the next hitter, everyone in the jam-packed ball field knew that Otto's assistant had given orders to hit away. The grandstand expert wanted a big inning.

Palmer slashed at the first pitch. The Tigers up to that instant had stood down there tense and

Hello, Fenway Park!

motionless, looking from the press box like plastic figures on a cardboard field. As soon as the ball was hit, however, that infield exploded into action. Maloski had moved with the pitch. The Tiger second sacker ran in to field the grounder, while the shortstop sprinted for second. With a fast underhand flip the second baseman got the ball to his shortstop. That man took the peg, leaped high to avoid Maloski's spikes, and fired to first for a sizzling double play.

Howls poured down from the mob in the seats. But the rush of sound was not directed onto the field, nor at Otto. All of it cascaded upon the head of the luckless grandstand manager.

Lefty watched in amusement as Otto turned toward the man in the box seat, took off his cap, and bowed almost to the ground. Then Otto walked calmly into the dugout.

It was the most interesting event in an otherwise drab evening for Boston. The Sox lost the game, 11-6. Lefty heard one observer comment, "What this team needs is a match to put under all that power the Sox have but don't use."

"Amen!" said the speaker's companions.

They glanced curiously at Lefty as he walked out of the press box with Ed Bowler. He knew what they were thinking.

CHAPTER XV

SURPRISE FOR LEFTY

Detroit left town on the midnight train for New York, but that meant no rest for the Red Sox. Close on Tiger heels came the White Sox, surging toward the top for the first time in many years. In fact, at the moment they led the completely astonished American League by three games.

Otto Luber lost no time making Lefty feel at home. He introduced him to the Sox players next morning at breakfast. Everyone greeted Lefty in a friendly manner. The entire squad seemed free and easy, apparently forgetful of the defeat of the night before.

Lefty wondered if the team suffered with the common disease of complacency that sometimes afflicted veteran players. On paper, the Boston outfit was the most powerful aggregation in the major leagues. Why, then, weren't they grinding the opposition into the dust?

Otto took him to a seat in the hotel lobby. The Red Sox manager came to the point fast.

"I'm puttin' you right out there today," the stocky pilot said. "You'll bat fifth, behind Sparky Fisher. I know it's lower than your usual spot, but I think you'll do us the most good there."

Lefty thought, any place is a good spot, as long as it's on a big league team!

He got out to Fenway Park early. Batting practice pitchers already were there, and he had a chance to try his power. One thing was against him, as it was against Kewpie Dolan, left-handed siege gun of the Red Sox. That was, the right-field fence and right-center were the longest distances in the field. They ran from three hundred and eighty feet in right to four-twenty in right-center.

The left-field barrier, made to order for starboard hitters, was only three hundred and fifteen feet away. The so-called "chummy" left-field fence! It was loved by such rightie swatters as Sparky Fisher and Axe Osborne. The fence was thirty-seven feet high there, against only five feet in right field. But into the screen above the barrier went many a Red Sox home run ball.

The regulars began trooping onto the diamond. Kewpie Dolan stood behind the batting cage while Lefty drove out several steaming liners. Dolan nodded his head in approval.

"Nice work, Lefty," he said as the ex-Virginian stepped out of the cage.

Infield practice was a revelation. Never before had Lefty seen ground balls handled so smoothly. Fisher knocked down a hard grounder at third and got it off in a streak to Lefty. Yet, hard as the throw came, it landed in the crab-net as soft as a baby's toss.

Suddenly, after a few rounds to the infield, Otto Luber took a bat and ball. Facing toward third, he swatted the ball and yelled, "Get two!"

To Lefty's surprise, the hit, instead of going to Fisher at third, headed sharply toward first. Before he realized what happened, the pill streaked inside the bag into right field.

The diamond went quiet as an empty locker room. Otto appeared undisturbed, however, and quickly hit another ball toward shortstop.

"Get two!"

Johnny Palmer took the hopper, shovelled it to Doc Spencer on second. Doc whipped it in one motion to first base.

The cry came again. "Get two!"

This time Lefty was set for the play. The hit came screeching to his right. He got over there, trapped the ball, and pegged it to second. By now he had Dave Kimball's advice about the DP stamped indelibly into his brain. He pivoted quickly, raced for first, pressed his foot on the bag, and turned barely in time to catch the sizzling return. The quick chatter of the infield and Otto's yell of encouragement told him that the play had been well handled.

Minutes went by, the stands filled rapidly, and Chicago came onto the field for drill. Lefty sat in the dugout, watching and listening intently as the visitors went through their workout.

"That Del Austin!" someone said admiringly as the Chicago shortstop whipped the ball around. "Ain't he a beauty?"

"I like that Crale on second," Tony Maloski said. "He's only a half-pint; but oh, man! Can he play that position!"

"An' Cy Barnes. On the bases he runs with his head down an' travels like a rocket. One time I got in his way. Ouch!"

"Who's throwin' for the White Sox?"

"Dunno yet. Prob'ly Camp. 'Member him?"

A grunt carried through the dugout. Camp was a former Boston hurler. He'd work like blazes today, if he pitched, to beat his old mates.

The gong rang sharply, and the Red Sox spilled onto the field. Clapping and assorted yells came from the already filled seats. Lefty, trotting out to first base, felt nearly thirty thousand pairs of eyes fixed on him.

They worked out for five minutes, waiting for game time. Boston's famed east wind was entirely absent, and the late June sun burned pitilessly down on the hot field. The butterflies came under

Lefty's belt, as they always did the first time he played with a new team. This was the major league, the big show, the chance he had been waiting for since that distant afternoon when he had first signed a professional contract.

The announcer's voice came jumping out of the loud speaker. At the end of the Chicago lineup boomed the pitcher's name: *Camp!* Camp was a right hander. Not a good man for Lefty to meet in his first big league start.

Then came the Red Sox lineup. Loud cheers greeted the name of Kewpie Dolan, popular because of his friendly attitude with the home fans as well as for his hitting. Polite cheers followed the name "Tarbin." The critical fans waited to see. They had been disappointed too many times by new first basemen who were supposed to be standout players, but who faded away rapidly.

Del Austin, Chicago lead-off man, hit the first pitch to third base. Fisher fielded the ball easily and gunned the throw to first. Again it came in fast but soft. Lefty made the putout and tossed to Doc Spencer. Mild cheers came from the stands. The ice was broken, the butterflies were gone, and this was just another ball game. A big one, but played on a regulation diamond just like all the rest. Only the play was faster. Much faster.

Lefty came to bat in the second inning. Camp had retired all three men in the first, and Fisher flied out to open the second. Now Lefty stood in

Surprise for Lefty

the batter's box, his first time up in a major league game. Eddie Boy's voice came crisply from the third base coach's box: "Cream the first one, Lefty boy. Outta the park!"

He looked Camp over carefully. The veteran right-hander was quick, no doubt of that. The first pitch came in, a little wide he thought, and he let it go by. To his surprise, the umpire called it a strike. He started to protest, thought better of it, and kicked at the dirt with his cleats. He set himself for the next pitch.

Camp threw the same thing, but wider still. This time a ball. Now it had to be in there. He glanced down toward Otto at first base. The manager flicked an imaginary fly from his cheek. The sign meant Otto thought a strike would come in next. Be ready for it. Cream it if it's good.

Camp gave him a teaser that hung in the air, then broke down and inside. Lefty stepped back and lunged. He connected with the fat of the wood under the ball; and he felt the old thrill of a base hit as the sphere zoomed to the outfield. He was sure it was in there.

But you're in the big leagues now. The outfielders were there to choke off hits, and Carl Campbell in center galloped across the turf without letup. Lefty had undercut the pitch enough to give it a little height. Campbell needed no more, and he made a great running catch before the line fly could get past him.

The throw bounced out of Lefty's crab-net.

Surprise for Lefty

Otto hit him lightly on the seat of the pants as he went back to the bench.

"Nice try, kid. You got a good piece of the ball. Stay with 'er!"

The game dragged into the ninth, then the tenth, without a score. In the last of the tenth, with one out, Sparky Fisher poked a single through the box. Lefty dropped a nice bunt along first, sending Sparky to second. Camp passed Axe Osborne, and Doc Spencer singled over shortstop to bring the run in. Boston copped the series opener by a 1-0 shutout and gained a full game on the White Sox.

Having set up the winning run and played errorless ball in the field, Lefty felt satisfied with his first major league game. True, he had failed to hit in four attempts, but only once had he looked bad. That was when Camp struck him out with a sinker ball. Camp wouldn't do that again soon.

That evening he got one of the most pleasant surprises of his life. Western Union paged him in the lobby. When he opened the telegram, it read: "Congratulations, major leaguer! Best wishes and lots of base hits." It was signed, "Mom and Dad."

A glow went through Lefty. All during the past months he had not forgotten the folks in Idaho. He hoped that they, too, were thinking often of him. And now, for the first time really, his father had taken notice of his baseball career. Was the older man relenting in his strong dislike for the game? In time, would he become another fan? If so, Lefty felt that his triumph would be complete —to be a big leaguer and to win over his dad to a love of the game.

Next day the White Sox made it clear that their position at the top of the league was no fluke. They came to the park, as Eddie Boy remarked at the close of the second inning, with their hitting clothes on. In those two innings Chicago scored five runs, drove Shad Kenney to the showers, and held the Red Sox hitless.

The game went along more or less in that fashion for seven innings. Lefty got his first major league hit in the fifth, a double off the right field wall that scored Johnny Palmer. But as Chicago came to bat in the first of the eighth, they held a safe 7-2 lead.

Cy Barnes, fleet White Sox third baseman, led off. He hit Jumbo Warner's first pitch into deep left field. The clout would have been a homer, but it veered off into the left-field bleachers at the last moment for a long foul. Barnes let the next two pitches go by. Then, on the two-and-one count, he swung late and topped the ball toward the pitcher.

Warner fielded it well and tossed to Lefty for the putout.

Ordinarily the play would have been routine. But Barnes, digging head down for first with all his speed, hit Lefty in the ribs with his shoulder. The throw, just settling into the crab-net, bounced out. Lefty hit the ground hard with his seat.

Angrily he got up, grabbed the ball, and started for Barnes. Then he held his temper, remembered

Surprise for Lefty 203

that someone had mentioned Barnes' habit of running head-down into the bases, and decided to let it go. Right now it would not do to stamp himself as a sorehead. Some of the Boston scribes, digging into his past, already had mentioned examples of his quick temper.

An elderly man in the first-base boxes, however, had no intention of letting the incident pass. He yelled an insult at Barnes—who of course was safe on the play—and then turned to pour out his wrath on Lefty.

"Hey, Tarbin, ya bum, wassa matter with you? Are ya yella?"

Lefty glanced at the man, shrugged his shoulders, and tossed the ball to Warner. He started to go back to his position when the next words of the oldster caught him like a blow on the chin.

"Your old man woulda killed Barnes fer that. He played baseball like a man, not a pantywaist. Are you yella?"

Lefty stopped dead and gaped at the speaker. He could not believe his ears. His father a ballplayer? Nonsense! The old man was crazy. Slowly he trudged to the bag, mechanically took up his position against the base to be ready for a pick-off throw.

Barnes took a big lead. Warner snapped a fast pick-off throw. Lefty, his mind still in a fog from the old man's words, stopped the throw, but did not hold it. Barnes meantime had sprinted for second. By the time Lefty retrieved the ball and got it down to Johnny Palmer, Barnes was in there safe.

Lefty took a terrific going-over from the fans. Barnes scored later, and as the Red Sox walked off the field for their half of the eighth, the elderly occupant of the box seat yelled again at Lefty.

"Yore old man was a sorehead, but he was a ball player. Too bad you ain't one. I hear he won't own ya. No wonder!"

Had the tormentor been a younger man, Lefty—despite strict league rules against it—would have stepped over and punched him. Instead, he walked head down into the dugout. He played the rest of the game in a daze.

Boston dropped that game, and Lefty was afraid that as a result of his play during the last two innings, the Red Sox might drop him, too.

No one mentioned the Barnes happening in the clubhouse or at dinner. Later, however, Otto called Lefty into the lobby. Otto's face had a sober look. Eddie Boy was there too.

"Look, kid," Otto said. "We're going to get this business straightened out right away. I dunno a thing about your father, but we're going to find out, since it seems to bother you. Was he a ball player? Was that old man in the box seat right?"

Helplessly Lefty shook his head. "I don't know. I never thought so. He always seemed to hate the game. Didn't want me even to play in college."

"Well, Eddie an' me an' you are going to find out, right now. Let's go."

Still shaken, Lefty followed them out into the street. Otto flagged a taxi. Lefty couldn't hear the

Surprise for Lefty 205

directions Otto gave the driver. He did not care much anyway. He still could not fathom the elderly fan's remarks.

They rode down to Newspaper Row and stopped at the Boston *Journal*. Otto took them up a narrow flight of wooden stairs and into the room that Lefty guessed right away housed the paper's sports headquarters. A gray-haired old timer was sitting at a corner desk, reading the sports page.

"Hello, Jim," Otto greeted him. "You know Eddie Boy."

"Sure, sure, Otto. Hi, Eddie!"

"I want you to meet our new first baseman, Lefty Tarbin. Lefty, this is Jim Wayne. Jim's been writing baseball for about a hundred years."

Laughing, Wayne extended his hand. "Not quite a hundred, Otto. But almost!" Wayne's keen eyes went over Lefty in an appraising glance.

Otto plunged into the subject immediately. "Jim, we got a problem. Did you ever hear of an old-time ball player named Tarbin? Jack Tarbin. He musta played back before the American League was organized."

Wayne scratched his chin. "Tarbin, Tarbin," he mused. "I dunno. No, I don't think— Wait a minute." He hesitated. "There was a guy with the old Phillies, I 'member. He didn't stay long. In a fight almost every game, he was. One day he punched an umpire, then walked off the field, tore off his uniform, an' disappeared. Never came back. Never played ball again, so far's I know. At least, I never heard of him again."

Otto pounded his fist excitedly. His face glowed. Lefty hardly dared breathe.

Otto said, "Can you check that, Jim?"

"Sure. Let's go down to the morgue an' look in the files."

When they got there, Wayne thumbed through yellowed old copies of the *Journal*.

"Musta been about nineteen-twelve or thereabouts. I rec'lect I was just startin' to write, an' it was a little while before the first big war. Here, you check some of the Phillie lineups of these grapefruit league games. Here's one played in Sarasota against Providence."

Otto and Eddie scanned the box scores. His body covered with warm sweat, Lefty stood and watched.

"Nope," Otto said. "No Tarbin here."

"Nor here either," Wayne replied. He put back the faded copies. Lefty did not know whether he himself felt disappointed or not.

Eddie suggested, "Let's try nineteen-thirteen."

"That's what I'm after," Wayne grunted as he pulled out more *Journals*.

They hunted through the box scores again. Otto shook his head.

"No soap, I guess."

Suddenly Eddie let out a yell. "Whoopee! Here. See? First base for Philadelphia in a grapefruit game with Baltimore. March 28, 1913. First base, Tarbin. An' the guy got four hits!"

Surprise for Lefty 207

Feeling weak in his legs, Lefty looked around for a chair. He found one, and sat down. Otto continued the hunt, like a prospector chasing down a vein of silver.

Otto turned the pages slowly. His face lit up, then clouded again. Finally his questing eyes hesitated, stopped on a page, and he shouted, "Here it is, just like you said, Jim." His fingers jabbed at an item in the paper. "April third, 1913. Jack Tarbin punched an umpire, walked off the field, and disappeared!"

"I bet a million ballplayers have wanted to do that, one time or another," Wayne chuckled.

Holding up the paper and pointing to the page, Otto turned to Lefty.

"Here's a picture of the Phillie Jack Tarbin, alongside the story. Is that your dad?"

Amazement mingled with disbelief as Lefty stared at the faded old photograph. It was a younger Jack Tarbin, the face a little thinner. But the straightforward look, the firm chin, and the strong features of the man looking out from the page at him were those of his father, forty years ago.

Numbly he lifted his head. "Yes, that's my dad."

"That settles it," Otto said kindly. "What you want to do now?"

Lefty rubbed a hand slowly across his forehead.

"I think," he said softly, "that I want to go back to the hotel. I need a good night's sleep. If I can get it!"

CHAPTER XVI

GOOD-BYE, TARBIN TEMPER

LEFTY slept quite well, after all. The more he thought about his father's baseball career, the better he liked it. He felt sorry that his dad in a fit of anger had quit the game. But he knew how the old Phillie player had felt. Many a time Lefty wanted to do the same thing. Only by conquering that temper, inherited from his ball-playing father, had he succeeded in staying in the game.

In the morning, he knew what he wanted to do. He went downstairs, found Otto in the lobby, and spoke to him.

Otto nodded approvingly. At that moment Ed Bowler came by, and Otto repeated to him what Lefty had said.

Bowler said, "That sounds okay. Let the club take care of it, Lefty. You concentrate on your ball

Good-bye, Tarbin Temper

playin', and we'll fix up everything the way you want it." He winked at Otto and smiled.

Walking the short distance to Fenway Park later, Lefty saw how all the pieces in the picture fitted together. His dad, probably even more strong-willed and hot-tempered in his youth than he was today, had grown embittered with the game of baseball. To him, taking orders and having to accept umpires' decisions—decisions with which he sometimes violently disagreed—was much too bitter a pill to swallow. In disgust he suddenly gave up the game, brooded over his early frustrations, and finally developed an intense hatred for baseball and everything connected with it.

And now Lefty knew, too, why Tarbin senior never wanted his son to know the bitterness and defeat that may come to professional ballplayers. Yet the older man had underestimated the son's ability to take as well as to give. When he saw the kind of stuff his son really was made of—

Lefty felt as though a heavy load had been removed from his shoulders when he walked out on the ball field that day. He looked for the old fellow in the box seats, wanting to thank him for his unintentional favor. But the elderly fan was not there. Lefty got two booming doubles that day, and the Sox beat Philadelphia, 6-0.

That night Bowler came up behind him as he ate and whispered in his ear, "We got an answer to the telegram. He said yes. Thursday at noon."

Thursday at noon! Two days more. He played baseball those two days with such elation that on the first day he hit three for four, including two more doubles; and on the second, his eighth-inning homer into the right-field bullpen gave the Sox a 5-4 win over the Athletics.

Just about this time a letter came from Bobby Dale.

"I read about your promotion to the Red Sox," Bobby wrote, "and it made me feel great—almost as good as if I'd gone up to the majors myself! Joe Gates and I are still here in Seattle, playing our heads off to get called up. Maybe next year we will get our chance in the big leagues.

"I had a letter from Art Gray last week. He's still at Kansas City, but the New York Yankees have promised him a tryout at their camp next spring. I don't see how Art can miss, do you? He's one of the best fielders in the business, and he says his hitting is coming along.

"Not much other news about the old Roughneck gang. Vic Sedgman and Barnacle Bill Berry are with the Tigers, as you probably know. They belong up there all right. You'll no doubt see them in action. Better have that bat of yours honed up good!"

Lefty smiled as he put away the letter. He hoped with all his heart that the guys would all make the majors. Even though he did not relish the thought of batting against either Sedgman or Barnacle Bill!

On Thursday afternoon the Yankees came in for

Good-bye, Tarbin Temper

the opener of a three-game series. Lefty could not be at the airport to meet the plane, but Bowler promised to go. Then, at two o'clock when the important series began, Lefty's parents would be sitting in a first-base box seat, watching him for the first time in a major league game.

"Gus Berger's goin' for the Yanks today," Johnny Palmer growled. "Won't we ever get anythin' but left-handers to hit against?"

Lefty smiled. To him, a steady diet of southpaws would be happy living.

Anyone who wants to see a Red Sox-Yankees game in Boston has to get to the park early. This bright, sun-filled day was no exception, for by one o'clock every seat was filled. From a big crowd Lefty always got a mild attack of goose pimples, but as soon as he threw the practice ball around a few times, the goose pimples disappeared.

Otto, batting some practice balls to the infield, drove a hot grounder deep to the right of shortstop. Johnny Palmer faded back, trapped the ball before it went by, and shot a low, bullet-like throw to Doc Spencer on second. Doc wheeled and gunned the ball across to Lefty. A smattering of applause showed the spectators' appreciation of the fast practice play.

Lefty tried to keep an eye on the first-base box that he had reserved for his mother and father. Minutes passed by, two o'clock neared, and still the Tarbins did not appear. Mild worry came into his mind. Could anything have happened? They should be here by now.

He imagined a plane crash, a taxi accident on the way across the city, and other kinds of calamities. Sitting on the bench while the Yankee infield worked out was an agony of suspense.

Then the five-minute gong rang, and he ran onto the sunny field with the rest of the team. A mighty roar burst from the fans and swept over Fenway Park.

"Let's go, boys!" Johnny Parker yelled, slapping his glove as he trotted to his position.

Cozy Smith took the mound for Boston. Anxiously Lefty glanced over at the box seats. Still no Tarbins there.

The five minutes of drill flew past like one minute. Then, "Play ball!", and Jeep Jennings stepped to the plate for the Yankees.

Jennings drove a sharp grounder to third. Sparky Fisher fielded it cleanly and pegged to Lefty for the out. Ben Lucas, Yankee right fielder, flied out to center field, and Al Heinz fanned.

Lefty chafed as he sat in the dugout. Where were Bowler and the Tarbins? He looked on, worried, as Maloski skied out to left. Johnny Palmer drew a pass, and the stands began to show life. Cheers swept over the park as Kewpie Dolan ambled to the plate.

Dolan swung lustily at the first pitch and the ball roared toward first base. The first sacker managed

Good-bye, Tarbin Temper 213

to knock the screamer down. Then, with no chance to catch Palmer at second, he picked up the ball and stepped on first.

Lefty walked into the on-deck circle as Sparky Fisher moved up to bat.

"C'mon, Sparky, ride it over the fence!" Eddie Boy yelled from third.

Sparky drew a line near the plate with his bat. He rubbed his hands on the side of his pants, set his cleats firmly in the dirt, and faced Berger. Sparky had a wide stance, his left foot pulled toward third base while he faced toward the pitcher. It was unorthodox batting form; but even so, Fisher could give the ball a long ride.

The first pitch was in there. Sparky put all his weight behind the swing. He caught the ball low, however, and sent up a high foul near third. Dick Hadley squeezed it for the putout. Palmer held second.

As Lefty stepped briskly from the circle, he glanced over at the box seats. His chest pounded at what he saw. Just settling into the Tarbin box were two people, a middle-aged lady and a man. The man had on a wide-brimmed Panama hat. He was tall, broad-shouldered; and his long arms made him appear even taller as he helped the lady into her chair in the box.

Even from that distance, Lefty recognized the two immediately. His mother and dad!

He put everything he had into his swing as

Berger's fast ball zoomed in. He grunted in satisfaction as the white sphere headed for the outfield. Then he was digging in, head down, sprinting like mad for first.

Otto howled at him from the coach's box. "Keep goin', Lefty! Run, kid, run!"

The ball sailed over Ben Lucas' head in right center, deep toward a jag in the wall at the 390-foot mark. Lefty rounded second still in high gear as he saw the ball strike the barrier and bounce crazily toward right field. Desperately Lucas put on the brakes, tried to change his direction. One knee slipped to the ground, and he lost precious seconds going after the hit.

High-balling it for third, Lefty tried with all his might to summon more speed. Anxiously he watched for Eddie Boy's signal. He expected the slide sign.

But Lucas must be eating that ball. Eddie kept waving his arms in wide circles. Keep going, Lefty! Take it all the way!

His feet grew heavy, as though someone had fastened weights to his ankles. His breath came in quick, searing gasps. He swept over third, bent his head, and high-tailed it for home. An inside-the-park home run? Maybe. If he could make it! The yells of the fans beat down on him as he ran, and he had a glimpse of Rocky Dawson blocking the plate. Rocky—squat, bull-like, and determined. It would be like trying to move a ten-ton truck to knock him away from the plate.

He left his feet far out from Dawson and came in with a bone-jarring slide. He heard the ball slap into leather as Lucas' desperate throw came all the way in on the first hop. Then, as he lay sprawled over the plate, with Dawson untangling himself from the pile, he saw the thumb of umpire Hal Iker jerk up sharply.

Out!

Hot blood rushed to Lefty's cheeks. He sprang to his feet and shoved his chin up against the umpire's jaw.

"You—you're crazy!" he screamed. "I was in there before he tagged me! Are you blind?"

Iker snarled, "You're out!"

Lefty pushed up against him. He knew he was losing control of himself, was blowing his top in the old Tarbin manner, but he could not stop. He hardly realized what he was screeching at Iker.

The umpire said again, shortly, "Out!" A dangerous look came into his eyes.

Lefty stepped all over Iker's feet. In another instant he would have shoved the blue-clad figure backward.

Then, for some reason, he looked over Iker's shoulder toward the first-base boxes. In a quick glance, he saw his father standing upright in the box, one fist held high and tightly clenched. His father was shouting, but there seemed to be something of pleading in his attitude, instead of wild anger.

Quickly then, something loosened inside Lefty.

He saw in retrospect his father's sudden, angry departure from baseball those long years ago; the bitter resentment over the intervening time; and now the older man's reborn interest in a game he once had loved so well.

And with all that, Lefty in a flash realized that now he could govern his own fiery temper. He did not need the restraining hands of Otto, nor the soothing "Take it easy, kid!" of Eddie Boy.

Abruptly he turned away from Iker and walked toward the dugout, slapping the dirt off his pants and stockings as he went. He sat down on the bench and folded his arms as he watched Otto and Eddie, who were still arguing with Iker.

Finally Otto gave up the dispute. Dawson's tag retired the side, and the Sox moved out to take the field again. Palmer scored on the play, at least, and Boston had a 1-0 lead.

When he stood once more on infield dirt, Lefty again thought of his father. He glanced quickly toward the box seats. His parents were intently gazing in the direction of first base. Lefty wondered what his dad really thought of the rhubarb at the plate. As he raised his glove in a brief signal of recognition, he saw his dad smile broadly, lift both hands clutched together, and wave them in a sign of approval.

Lefty felt a thrill of satisfaction in the realization that at last his father understood. There would be no more coldness between them, he knew, because of Lefty's baseball career.

Good-bye, Tarbin Temper

The game moved through the second, third, and fourth innings without a score. In the fifth, Swede Gustaffson led off with a single that Lefty just missed fielding. Then the Yanks put on the hit-and-run. Dick Hadley drove one through the open second-base slot as Doc Spencer moved to cover second.

With two men on, Russ Weber doubled over Axe Osborne's head in right. Two runs came in, but Weber was nabbed trying to make third on the play. The next two batters flied out, leaving New York with a 2-1 lead.

Boston tried hard to even the count in its half. But though catcher Louis Hoff and Tony Maloski got on base, they died there when Palmer and Dolan flied out. Dolan took a rough going-over from the fans after failing to produce a hit.

Someone muttered, "The way Berger an' Smith are goin', it looks like nobody will ever score again."

Otto overheard the remark. "Don't talk like that!" he rasped, a cold light showing in his eyes. "You guys shake it up. Get some runs, see? We can pull this game out yet!"

The sixth inning passed, and the seventh, still without further scoring. Every fan in the park stood up for a lucky seventh, but the Sox could not even get a runner on base.

They threatened in the eighth. Cozy Smith got a pass and Palmer sacrificed him to second. Then Maloski drove a screaming line drive that appeared headed for left center. But Jeep Jennings leaped high in the air and pulled off a miracle catch with his gloved hand.

Smith, feeling certain the drive would get past Jennings, started for third. When he saw the catch, he tried frantically to get back to second, but stumbled. Jennings threw to Russ Weber for an easy double play.

An audible groan wafted down from the stands. Otto came in to the bench seething.

"What a break!" he stormed. "Those Yankees always play with horseshoes in their pants." He glared down the length of the dugout. No one was in a mood to dispute him.

After a break like that, New York tried to pour it on for a big inning. It was typical Yankee strategy, to steamroll the other team when it was dragging its heels in discouragement.

Rocky Dawson led off for the Yanks. He pumped a Texas Leaguer to center. Lefty, backed up against first base to hold the runner on, knew the rumbling Dawson never would attempt a steal. The play had to be another hit-and-run.

He saw Rube Nelson flash a sign to Swede Gustaffson at the plate. Swede swiftly glanced away, tugging at his cap. Then he place-hit the first pitch to Lefty's right. Swede had tried to hit the slot which Doc Spencer left open as he moved to cover second.

Thinking ahead of the Yankees, Lefty anticipated

Good-bye, Tarbin Temper

the play. As soon as Smith loosed his pitch, Lefty moved to his right. The batted ball spurted toward the gap in the Sox infield. But it was not far enough over. Lefty reached out his crab-net and speared the racing pellet. His throw beat Dawson to second by yards. Then he turned and sprinted back to first.

He had time to get there before Swede did. But could he whirl around fast enough to catch Doc's swift return? Feeling more nervous than he ever had on a diamond before, he thrust his foot on the bag and wheeled in one motion. He saw Doc's throwing arm already down, the ball flying through the air in his direction. His glove came up just in time to snare the sizzling peg. Swede's foot hit the bag an instant too late.

Lefty did not need the wild, approving yells of the crowd to know that it was a good play. Split-second timing alone had made it possible. He thought gratefully of the fielding advice that Dave Kimball had given him at Richmond.

That play killed Yankee hopes for a fat inning. Dick Hadley lofted a long fly to left, and the Bronx Bombers were retired.

The Red Sox came in jabbering with determination.

"Waddya say, guys?"
"Get them runs back!"
"We can do it."
"We *gotta* do it!"

Johnny Palmer grabbed his favorite war club.

"I'll get on," he growled, "if I have to go out there and skull Berger with this bat!"

He did not have to skull the Yankee hurler. Berger ran the count to three and two. Then he tried to sneak a fast one by Johnny; but the Boston shortfielder smacked it over third for a hit.

Otto gave Kewpie Dolan the bunt sign. Lefty knew the husky outfielder hated to lose a chance to hit, especially with a run on base. But Dolan laid one nicely along the first-base line, putting Johnny on second.

Lefty moved on deck as Sparky Fisher went to bat. The park was a bedlam, with so much noise coming from the stands that Lefty scarcely could hear the umpire's ball-and-strike calls.

Sparky missed the first pitch by a mile. The second was too wide. Berger came in next with a sinker. Sparky topped it, sending a high bounder to Jennings. The Yank shortstop paused momentarily after fielding the hopper, to keep Johnny on second. Then he whip-lashed his peg to first in time.

Two outs, the Red Sox trailing by one run, and Lefty Tarbin at bat.

He did not dare glance down the line at his dad. All he saw, as he set himself at the plate, was the ominous form of Berger on the mound. He had hit Berger for a triple, almost a homer, in the first. But the shrewd portsider never would give him the same pitch again. Lefty did not believe that Berger would put his fast ball anywhere near the plate this time.

Good-bye, Tarbin Temper

He was correct. Berger came in with a fast one, all right. But it was a duster. Lefty fell back just in time to escape being hit. The mob yelled angrily, and Lefty saw Otto shake his fist menacingly at Berger. But Otto did not leave the coaching box, and Berger ignored him.

Johnny danced on the basepaths, hoping to upset Berger. The unruly mob tried to rattle the Yankee pitcher, too, with catcalls and a rhythmic chanting.

"Take the bum out! Take Berger out!"

Berger, too crafty a veteran to be panicked so easily, stood silently on the mound. He nodded as Dawson gave him a signal.

The pitch came in, heading straight for Dawson's outflung mitt. In a lightning flash, Lefty remembered how Fisher had topped Berger's sinker. It would be fatal to hit the same type of ball. Any infielder would gobble it up.

He let the serve go by. It dropped sharply. Hal Iker droned, "Stee—*rike!*" and flung up his right arm.

Berger gazed toward the plate impassively. What were he and Dawson thinking? Most likely, they figured that Lefty would not be fooled again by the same pitch. Well, Lefty thought grimly, that was just what he wanted them to think. He had not been fooled the first time. He could have hit the sinker. But he knew he could not give it the height and distance he needed.

Berger teased him with a wide curve. Ball two. The next one should be in there. Berger would not make it too good. Probably another curve that would drop off the table, too wide for Lefty to clobber against the fence. Or so the Yankee hurler would think.

Lefty glanced down toward Eddie Boy. Eddie quickly brushed his fingers across his belt buckle. It was the sign that Eddie, too, expected the curve. Maybe he had caught Rocky Dawson's signal.

Well, Lefty reflected tightly, this is it. He set himself for the curve.

Berger took no wind-up. He kept the corner of his eye warily on Palmer. The latter danced like a dervish off second, yelling insults at Berger and encouragement to Lefty.

Eddie Boy shouted, "Knock this rube's block off, kid!"

Then Berger reared back. His front leg went high in the air. His left arm came down in a wide arc, his wrist snapping off the ball at the last split second. It was like a teamster cracking his bullwhip off the lead horses' shoulders.

The white sphere came down the alley with express-train speed. It headed for the far corner of the plate. Lefty gauged its speed, the probable amount and the instant of its dip. He never took his eyes off the ball. Every ounce of strength went into the swing as he brought the bat around. The ball dipped sharply, and in a brief, terrible flash Lefty thought his timing was off.

Then he felt the impact of ash upon horsehide.

He leaned heavily into the ball, and then gave his wrists all the twist he could muster. In that moment he knew he had caught the curve solidly.

Deafening roars came from thirty thousand throats as the ball arched skyward. Joy flowed through Lefty as he dug his spikes into the dirt. The foul line flew beneath him. He watched the flight of the ball, saw it curve sharply from left center up and toward the netting above the left field fence.

As he rounded first, hearing faintly Otto's "Atta boy, Lefty!" over the bedlam of crowd noise, he glanced up again. The long ball was just settling easily into the netting.

It was good, the warm feeling that came over him as he rounded the base paths. The rhythmic pounding of his feet on the infield dirt ran up through his body, and his heartbeat was a soothing throb in his breast. Jeep Jennings already had shoved his mitt in his back pocket and was trudging disconsolately from the field. Dick Hadley, Yankee third sacker, still had his eyes glued as if in disbelief on the far left field barrier. Then he, too, slowly turned and walked away.

"Yea, Lefty! Yea, Tarbin!" The shouts came from high in the third-base grandstand. The noise was a deep-throated roar, and Lefty knew that in this supreme moment he was the prince of Fenway Park.

Eddie Boy slapped his pants as he went by. He jogged happily into home plate, where Johnny waited to grab his hand. Then the whole Sox squad was crowding noisily about him.

"Wow, Lefty! You did it!"

"Oh, you Lefty! Lemme at him."

"Where's that-there pennant, guys?"

"Yea! Who's gonna stop us now?"

Eager hands slapped his back. He tried to get away, headed as fast as he could for the dugout.

As he touched his cap to the shrieking mob behind the Sox bench, he shot an eager glance down toward the box seats opposite first base. In the fleeting glimpse he had, he saw a middle-aged lady jumping up and down in the enclosure, clapping her hands wildly. Beside her, a tall, broad-shouldered man with long arms waved a Panama hat. He, too, was screeching madly, obviously a willing victim of the hysteria that gripped Fenway Park.

The last thing Lefty saw as he stumbled down the dugout steps was the broad-shouldered man throwing his Panama high into the air and giving out with another roar of joy.

Gosh, this is great! It's sure great to be a major leaguer and one of the Red Sox!

Who's gonna stop us now?